Joining a dating app is never the start of a fairytale--
I had known that from the beginning. So by no account did I expect to watch as this strong, handsome, sun-kissed God strolled into my life. Ever since Greg appeared on my phone, everything's changed. Those ocean blue eyes, his strong, fit, muscular arms—he's magnetic—and I can't stop myself from being pulled closer into his world. It was never supposed to be this way: him and me. I am so helplessly ordinary, and he is so eternally mesmerizing—and he wants me.

   I've tried to understand it. I've sought to see myself the way that he sees me—as if I am truly the goddess he desires. I've been hurt before. I'm not ready for this. Yes, I crave the thought of his hands, his lips, his dominant body. He is hypnotic, and I am his willing victim. Whatever this is—whoever he is—I'm in far too deep to turn back now.

Billionaire Blind Date
Fans of J.S. Scott, Penny Wylder, and E.L. James will love the fun, sexy style of Elyse Young. A fun and naughty read for the vixen in all of us!

Thank you for reading!

If You like my work, please take a minute to write a review.

Visit my website and sign up for exclusive content, updates and FREEBIES!

ELYSEYOUNG.COM

Copyright © 2016 by Elyse Young

All rights reserved. No part of this publication may be reproduced, distributed, or transmitted in any form or by any means, including photocopying, recording, or other electronic or mechanical methods, without the prior written permission of the publisher, except in the case of brief quotations embodied in critical reviews and certain other noncommercial uses permitted by copyright law. For permission requests visit elyseyoung.com

Chapter One

I grimace at my reflection. Damn my fair skin, now overly flush, making me look like I just been on a run. I wonder if this 'Greg' has ever been on a date where the person you meet looks entirely different from the pictures. Well, that's exactly what's about to happen. I sigh to myself. Don't get me wrong; I look ok. I just photograph very well. Too well really. It's not like I manipulate the pictures at all. But, I can't help but be nervous right now. I'm fidgeting with my top, as I wait, not so patiently at a coffee shop on the tip of Beverly Hills for my blind date to arrive.

I can't believe I'm doing this. I shake my head at myself. I'll just have to wait and see whether Jennifer is getting thank you muffins tomorrow, or the cold shoulder.

My mind wanders back to a week ago when I minded my own business, and as usual Monday mornings are, Jennifer was raving about her fabulous 22-year-old life and her weekend on the town. I had thought to myself, 'to be young and beautiful!' Inwardly I sighed. I've never been young or beautiful.

Oh well, at 31, I'm working with what God gave me, and feeling like I'm getting to a point in my life where I'm closer to at peace about my body. 5'9", tall for a girl, pasty white skin with a sprinkling of freckles across the bridge of my tiny nose. I blame it on my heritage on the Irish side. I like to think of myself as only slightly, pleasantly plump but probably could use a workout or 10, a dirty kind of green eyes and boob's just a bit too small... The one thing I feel is to my benefit is my hair. It's thick and curly and a bit on the long side. My red hair has streaks of a golden red, which of course, I was teased about mercilessly when I was younger. Now, however, I have grown to love it, and I feel like my hair is my shining glory. So, of course on Monday, when Jennifer was buzzing about her fabulous weekend on the town, I must've mumbled to myself that if I had her looks, I might be out on the town as well. Purely to myself of course. She leaned in close to me, sharing with me that she was having fun, this week at least, because of a "cool new dating app."

"Oh, I don't know much about that kind of stuff." I dismissed the idea quickly. "Isn't it scary meeting people you don't know?"
"Get with the program Kaitlin!" she playfully nudged my shoulder.
"It's safer than ever. Your profiles are rated, you meet in public first. And more importantly" her eyebrows wag suggestively. "It's a fun way to meet tons of super cute guys!"
"I don't know…"
She must have sensed my interest, as she quickly whipped out her phone and hopped on the counter of our station in the dressmaker's shop where we work.
"Come on Kaitlin! It's so easy even you could do it!" She laughed to herself as if what she said is funny. Her baby blue painted fingernails glided across her phone in a frenzy as she began to flip through something like a digital catalog filled with some pretty attractive guys. Ok, some, not so much as well. But still, it seemed like an interesting thing to pass the time with one night, maybe.
"It's called 'Mage,'" she said gleefully. It favorites for you and when there's a match you get a heart in the box here. You can still chat with whoever you like, or you can fill out

information about yourself to get better matches." She said, almost in passing. "I mean if you're looking for a relationship or whatever. But for a fun night out, it's the only app I use now! It's crazy fun! I have met so many cool people because of it. I met a DJ just last week who took me to a secret underground rave. Which was really underground! I mean, we were let into a section where I think they were building part of the subway expansion. Anyways, Kaitlin you should totally check it out." She pauses momentarily, eyes glazed, thinking of something naughty, most likely. "You need to get out there and have some fun girl! I haven't seen you with a guy for as long as I've known you. Who knows,if you don't use it it might just seal itself shut." hair hazel eyes twinkled with merriment as she pinched my leg playfully.
I laughed begrudgingly.
"Fun doesn't sound like a bad idea." As much as I hated to admit it, I was desperately lacking in that department recently. I can admit to myself that after my ex, I'm damaged goods and not ready to jump into any relationship, but as she continued to flip through the pictures of the supposed eligible bachelors, I couldn't help but notice some gentlemen more in my age group. As I went through the rest of my work day, my mind kept wandering over the guys in the app as she flipped through.
Then at lunch, the little pixie manhandled me and took my phone, batting at my hands when I thought to try to get it back. I watched in horror and excitement and a jumble of feelings I couldn't quite process at the time as she took it upon herself to download this "Mage" dating app. She then went through my phone and picked through pictures of me flipped through pictures of me.

"No, No, No. None of these will do! Here, Smile!" and she snapped a stunned picture of me. I was so stunned, in fact, that I didn't think to hide my face. She flashed the phone in my direction and said "There, perfect! Now, for your profile. What should we say? Oh, I got it! 'A homebody dressmaker looking for someone to show me how fun the city can be!' How old are you again Kaitlin? 31, right? Dressmaker and... Hmm...what do you like to do for fun? I see you every day, and I don't know." The bubbling babbling brook suddenly stilled in contemplation, tapping the phone to her chin.

"I like to do lots of things." I crossed my arms in defense. "I am NOT just, a homebody!" I almost yelled... "I like to read. I watch movies. I... I make designs for new dresses I think of sometimes. Okay, okay. I see your point I do need to get out. But I can setup on my own profile. Thank you very much!" I gingerly pulled my phone from her helpful clutches. Later that night I was so excited, having decided in my mind and in my daydreams to go ahead and give it a try. No expectations, Just to meet new people. So I filled out information about myself, trying, to be honest but not too honest, and talking about what two things I like to do for fun. And then begin to browse through the virtual supermarket of men. Young, old, big, small, tall, hippie, professional, dirty thug. I didn't do any flipping or bookmarking or anything like that. Just as Jennifer had explained, the software in the app was tracking my eyes movements and noting who it thought I liked. So I played with my phone for an hour letting the phone flip through men, feeling like a teenage girl flipping through a 'Teen Bop' or 'Tiger Beat' at pictures of the teen heartthrobs, oohing and ahhing. It dawned on me sadly after about an hour or so of playing with the guy's pictures that no one had responded to my posting. Just like real life, I guess, I sighed to myself. I closed the app and turned on the television deciding on a rerun of a modeling reality show. As I immersed myself in the problems of the teenager's 'pretty girl' problems, I felt almost a light bulb moment. Red-hot anger boiled beneath my skin. At 31, I'm not dead yet! Yes, I might not be a 19-year-old supermodel wannabe, but I'm good looking. Ish. I'm always getting compliments on my hair. And I'm smart! And fun to be around. My work crush, Josh is always walking by and pulling my hair, which I'm pretty sure is his way of work flirting. So, taking a deep breath to steel my gumption, I reached back to my side and picked up my phone opening the app again... As I was roaming through the magic dating app, just looking through the pictures. As if by magic, the floodgates opened and I started getting bombarded with messages from quite a few guys, generally with the all powerful and oh so alluring line of, "Sup girl!?".

Really? That's your opening line, guys? I'm sure they send that to everybody, and I hope to see what happens with it. I guess dating has evolved while I've been in hiding. And not for the better. But my problem was that I wasn't getting any interest from people who I can see myself dating, or even flirting with, for that matter. So I started looking around in earnest and decided to be a little bold and maybe message a couple of guys myself. I bit my lip wearily as I thought back to the dating Bible remembering "the rules"... that us good girls aren't supposed to ask guys out. I've been on this earth for 31 years, and I know that there's a little bit of truth to that. When you ask a guy out, you become the aggressor and lose a little bit of your power. I find myself attracted to manly men, the aggressive type, and the pursuers. I like to feel pursued, just to feel attractive and see that somebody found something sexy or attractive about me. But when you're asking a guy out, well, that's all she wrote, I've said to myself and friends many a time. "Men are like dogs. They do exactly what you allow them to." I shuddered to myself thinking of the unhappy memories of my ex, Daniel. "So you better take the time and train them right." So I was very brave and slightly stupid... I think to myself now, when I took the initiative to scroll through the pictures of the handsome men who weren't messaging me and ask some questions and say hello in a flirty way. No response generally speaking but... What the heck I thought. It's like practice. After a while, I decided just to 'go for broke,' act like I am Miss Hot Stuff and message everybody I think is cute and just have fun with it. Message to my heart's content because apparently these guys are not paying attention or interested or all of the above so why not have some fun with it. I sat up in my bed that night in front of the television, eating chocolate chip cookies, drinking red wine, with my hair all over my head. I looked atrocious, but I felt sexy as I messaged every cute guy within a hundred mile radius. I felt like a teenage girl unleashed. It started small. I messaged a guy named Boblovesgolf1978. A man whose picture looked to me, like maybe he was a lawyer who enjoyed a game of golf on the weekends. My message was simple, 'Hi! I'm new here. Any advice?' Definitely not a flirty tone, but reaching out a hand to shake it and introduce myself. "Hi, Kaitlin. Welcome to the magic land." He replied back simply. "my advice to you is have fun, and be safe. Beautiful hair btw." That was it. No sort of love connection, but a friendly soul. It was just enough to spur me. Time just flew! I messaged everybody! I flirted relentlessly. I had fun and commented on guys who I would never in a million years in real life go up to or flirt with in a restaurant, or bar, or anywhere. And, guess what? I fell into a good conversation with a hot guy... Who would have thought? After the barrage of "sup girls" from weirdo's, my night has quietly transformed!

 Now about Greg. Supposedly, he's 6'4", with blonde hair and ocean blue eyes and a gorgeous tan, European background which I love, and the most beautiful lips I have ever seen on a man. All of his pictures he is smiling a dazzling white smile with beautifully straight teeth. (Oddly, almost all of his pictures were very grainy.) He works at a bank, but he says his job it's boring. He has two cats and a dog, no kids, never married, loves comedy. Well, I laugh to myself, we'll see how much of this is true when I finally meet him. Now, here is where I feel a little uncomfortable. In most of these pictures, he's doing all these wild activities like climbing a mountain or skiing or out by the beach, and I am what would be referred as "indoorsy." We tested for ages, feeling like fast friends, about books and movies and food, things we enjoy to do, through the safe embodiment of the application of course. We had been texting for about an hour when he asked if he could call me. I thought for a minute nibbling on my bottom lip. Hmm, what would that be like? I thought to myself, Hey, I'm just having some fun. This will never go anywhere. So why bother? My inner pragmatic monster hissed. Another little voice in the back of my head said why not? You don't have to meet him. What would you like to hear the sound of his voice? I grinned and typed yes. I'm so he texted me his number, and I texted him mine and waited, nervous for him to call. He called immediately. Wow.

"Kaitlin?" Purred a strong soft voice that I immediately knew to be Greg.

"Greg?"

"Wow. Your voice is... Better than I could ever hope." I think to myself his voice is like melted butter dripping all over my skin. It is so warm and soothing. "You called so quickly."

"Well, I like to think of myself, as a man of action. I prefer to talk to you and see you in person than type, type, type away. I feel like a lot of the people on here can be really…" He hesitates, searching for the right word, "Flaky..."

"Well, I agree. You're the first person I've talked on the phone from here, I just recently joined, you see. I'm a little nervous. So I don't know if people can be flaky but, I haven't met too many interesting folks yet."

"Well, I feel honored." His laugh is electric. "What made you decide to say yes? "

"Honestly?" I'm sure I'm flushed red from smiling. Golly, flirting is fun!

"I prefer honesty, Kaitlin. In all things. I hope you do too."

"Well…" I think for a minute, measuring my words. "You seem genuinely nice."

"Oh no!" he laughs woundedly. "Not nice! That's the worst thing you could say to a guy like me. Guys don't like to be nice. I need something to boost my ego." My inner pragmatic's hackles rise.

"If you need an ego boost, Greg, I think you're talking to the wrong girl." It felt weird grinning like a school kid.

"Well, I guess when talking to a girl as beautiful as you. I'll let that be enough of an ego boost for me. I'm glad you're talking to me, Kaitlin. So when am I going to get to meet you?" I cringe at the compliment. Wow! Now here is a guy who gets to the point. I wanted to say the same thing from the beginning of the call, but I thought it would be too forward. In truth, I hate to type. And I feel like I'm an auditory person, so the sound of his voice was really turning me on.

"Well, if you don't mind. I'd love to have another conversation with you before we meet. Just to make sure."

"Like a phone date? "

"Well, I've been out of the loop. What's a phone date?"

"Kind of like what we're doing but we set aside a time to do it and we have a long conversation."

"As long as it doesn't end with any happy ending I'll be okay with that." I smiled to myself.

"I thought girls liked a happy ending?" He said ignoring my double entendre.

"Okay, well," I yawn "We've been chatting and texting and talking for 3 hours now, and I have to get up and go to work in the morning." There's a bit of a silence, and I think he feels as though I've rejected him.

"Can I call you tomorrow?" he says almost shyly." "I'd like that." My voice becomes breathy as I smile into the phone.

"Goodnight." I can feel his warm grin through the phone.

"Goodnight."

"Until tomorrow."

And so, we went on not one, but three phone dates. Tuesday, Thursday, and Sunday, and we talked about all sorts of things. We probably talked for more than 10 hours, if you added them all together. I can't think I've spent that much time talking to any man in my life. Not even my father. I blush remembering our first call. His voice was so outrageously sexy. I was almost dreading the inevitable meeting in real life.

As I was having such a good time, it was bound to be a disappointment. But what if, huh?

At five pm on the dot on Tuesday, my cell phone buzzed, causing a rush of excitement to course through me. I had saved him as a favorite in the app and was excited when the phone rang, and I saw it was him on the caller ID.

"Hello?" Was that my voice? My voice sounds so breathy and light.

"Hey. It's Greg." His voice is like a warm bath. Once it hits my ears, it warms my whole body.

"Of course it is. I'm happy you called." I have to make an effort to breathe. I'm far too excited for just a phone call with a practical stranger.

"You're surprised? I thought we had a date scheduled…" I can't tell if he's amused or upset. I can't help but sense that he is slightly offended at my hello.

"I guess I'm new, but I sense that people are a bit flaky on this app. I did tell you that you're the only person I've even slightly connected with on here right?"

"And I hope I'll be the last." his grin is audible, and as it turns out, contagious. There is an energy to Greg's voice that has me tingling all over.

"Are you at home?" I search frantically for something to say. I'm really not good at small talk.

"Yes. You?"

"I got off an hour ago. How was your day at work?" I'm typically at work till 5 or 6, but took off a bit early wanting to unwind a bit before our 'phone date'. Though still nervous, the pot of coffee I've brewed and the bottle of wine uncorked in front of me serve as armor. I cuddle on the couch with a blanket, Indian style, and the phone is on speaker.

getting me naked as soon as possibly possible. Grabbing his waist I tug at his shirttails, admiring the way his muscles indent at his hips, making a sexy v that leads to my happy place. In my haste, I accidentally pop one one his buttons. It flies across the room, knocking over some sort of greeting card. Now we are both laughing and kissing and naked. Oh, my!

Kissing me one last time, Greg gets up and heads to his dresser, searching for something. When he returns he's holding several silk scarves.
"Can you trust me enough for this?"
"Enough for what, exactly?"
"Enough to play a game that ends in you screaming my name?" He smiles now, rubbing the scarves gently across my skin. Still, though, I can tell that he is nervous. He waits with baited breath for my approval. It's his hesitation that makes my decision easy. I know that he would never do anything to hurt me. A little voice in the back of my head reminds me that I have thought that before. I tell my inner coward to shut up.
"You'll stop if I say?"
"I'll stop if you say lollipop." Lollipop? "You have to trust me to push you a little bit further…" his sentence dwindles, as he scratches his nails down my leg, hard, causing a rush of pain. His strong fingers then soothe it, so very softly drawing patterns on my suddenly sensitive flesh.
"I trust you enough."
"Thank you." With those words, he reaches up and covers my eyes with silk. Next comes my hands strapped to the bedpost. Then, my ankles are tied to the corners of the bed

leaving microscopic wiggle room. I am spread wide, naked, vulnerable and sightless. After I am secure, he begins touching me all over, Light gentle strokes, soothing my skin. He kisses my belly button.

"I'll be right back." He whispers into my mouth, almost, but not quite kissing me. And suddenly he is gone. The room is quiet, with only the sound of a waterfall in his backyard in the distance. He's gone to what seems like ages. I imagine what I must look like completely spread out on this lavender silk sheet. My arms and legs bound and spread far apart. My eyes covered. My gold-red hair fanned out across the bed. My fair skin, now blotchy and red, from being so overheated and aroused. My heavy breath causing my chest to rise and fall quickly. I test my bonds and think they are unyielding. Just as I feel the slow creep of fear from being exposed and trapped, he returns. I cannot see him, but I can sense him. Doesn't he know that he has an energy that commands any room? He is moving silently. I'm sure he hopes that I can't see or hear him. Is he studying my vulnerability? He is deceptively graceful as he floats across the room to the bed, hovering above me, without touching me. He is very near my face. So near now in fact, that I can feel the heat coming off of his skin. He comes closer still. Almost of the point to where we are touching. My breathing becomes more rapid. My chest is heaving so strongly now, that my nipples just, just graze his chest. I smile.

"You are so beautiful." he kisses me deeply.

Soft Spanish jazz starts. I'm focusing on my breathing, trying to calm my frantic nerves.

His first touch startles me. So soft and light, it's unexpected... he begins stroking up and down my body with soft languorous

"The usual. My job is mainly to make sure everyone else is doing their job. But I don't want to talk about my job. Honestly, I fell into it and am a bit stuck."

"So you don't really like it?" That doesn't quite make sense with what I know of Greg. He seems like such a tenacious person. It doesn't make sense that he would have a job that he didn't love. There is a brief silence, and I can tell he is trying to choose his words carefully.

"It's a family tradition. Both my father and his father were bankers so it… was expected of me. And it turns out I'm good at it. Plus," he changes the subject nervously, "It affords me time for fun. I often take days off to hike, ski, surf. In a perfect world, right?" I can tell this is a sensitive subject. I feel sad for him for a moment that he hates his job.

"I guess I'm lucky then. I'm a dressmaker, and I like my job. I just work for a small boutique shop now, but sometimes we do dresses for celebrities and the like…" another awkward pause. "So I guess no business talk then." I'm very nervous, and I feel like I'm babbling.

"Okay," he agrees.

"So what do you like to do for fun? Besides all that outdoorsy stuff. I'm afraid I'm not very outdoorsy." "That's okay. Maybe we could start slow? Have you ever been on a hike? It's just walking Outdoors."

"Well, I am trying to get out more. That might be fun."

"I'll make sure it's fun." it feels like a promise like he's already planning the trip in his head. When he says it, I believe him.

"Any family?" Quite the change of subject, but okay.

"I have a mom and dad in another state. We don't really talk, though. You?"

"Unfortunately, both of my parents are dead. My father died when I was around 18. My mother just recently."
"I'm very sorry to hear that. Were you very close?"
"Not really. I spent most of my youth away at school. My friends were closer than any family."
"I understand. My parents had me later in life. I was kind of an accident. So they weren't really interested in having a child. Sadly I didn't really have a lot of friends growing up. Not until I was in high school."
"So, you became the social butterfly in high school?"
"Not really, but I dated a jock, so suddenly I was included in a lot of activities. I, myself was a nerd and bookworm."
"Bookworm, huh, sounds cute. Did you wear glasses?" He's teasing me now, I suspect.
"No, no glass. You've seen my pictures."
"Yes. You're beautiful." Beautiful? Really? Was he looking at my pictures?
"Not really. In fact, people made fun of my hair when I was younger. And now it's my best feature."
"You do have beautiful hair." The words come out sunken, almost a growl. "But I think you have a beautiful smile as well. So what are you doing right now?"
"Well, I'm talking to you!"
"I know, but what are you doing while I'm talking to me. I hope you're not on the site looking at other guys." A giggle escapes me.
"No, I get the feeling you're more than I can handle... I brewed a pot of coffee, and I've got a bottle of wine out. And I'm curled up on the couch with an afghan. All I need is a kitty to stroke, and I'd be the picture spinster." His laugh is rich and raw. I like the sound.

"You probably think this funny, but you just described me. Except I do have the cats. I'm sipping on a glass of cabernet. I have two kittens in my lap, Cinnamon and Charlie. Say hello boys." The phone slides from his face, and I can hear this light mewing and purring of kittens. "I also have a dog. It's a girl named Honey. She's quiet now, though. Partially tuckered out from our run awhile ago. She's half asleep. But I'm very much an animal person.I often volunteer at a no-kill shelter. That's where I got Honey. What about you?"
"I love animals!" I exclaim. "This apartment just does not allow them, unfortunately. What kind of kittens are they?"
"Calicos. A friend of mine I had a litter and I couldn't help myself."
"They sound just adorable…"

We talked for hours. And hours again the next day, and the next.
So when he finally asked me out, Sunday, yesterday night...
"Are you ready yet, Kaitlin? Can I see you tomorrow.?" I felt that there was a sense of urgency and longing in his voice.Well, I thought to myself. I guess the jig is up. It was fun while it lasted, anyway.
"Well," I couldn't help but feel deflated for a moment. "I'm worried that if we do meet, we might not like each other in real life."
"I told you from the beginning, Katy, I'm a man of action. I'm not here to meet a new friend. I'm here to meet someone special. I think you've got the potential to be someone really special to me. Where would you like to go?" Just like that. The question was no longer if, but where and when. He was

good. He was so sure of himself. The thought of someone with that much charm makes me hot and tingly, and also screams 'Danger! Danger, Will Robinson!'
"How about we meet for coffee?" I tried to think of the most harmless settings possible
"Coffee sounds great!"

We both worked in the morning, so we set a date to meet at the Coffee Shop on 3rd and La Cienega at 7 p.m., and now I'm here. Trying to fix myself up to look as much like my photos as possible. They're all current photos too. So, why am I so nervous.

Chapter Two

It's 6:55. I sit with a café Americano with a shot of sugar-free vanilla trying to get my energy up so I can seem excited instead of nervous. My hands are clammy. I hold the cup and revel in the warmth seeping in through my hands breathing deeply of vanilla and coffee and cream, trying to calm myself. I hear him before I see him. Hell, I sense him before I hear him. His presence is so strong. His small laugh to my right is warm as he holds the door open for slight young woman exiting, her arms filled with baked goodies. Maybe not him, though? This face does not match the pictures he had online. The features are similar but not quite right. Walking in now, he looks nothing like his photos... Yes, both are tall, strapping and beautifully formed. Is this him? He looks around the room and sees me. He smiles. I inhale deeply. I hadn't realized I've been holding my breath. I guess I've been waiting to see whether or not he approved. Of course, he could just be acting polite. And soon his phone will ring with some excuse to leave, I'm sure, in 10 minutes. I've been told I come off of it standoffish when people first meet me. Even good friends said that they thought poorly of me when we first met. "Kaitlin?" He calls out from the doorway, the voice like an old friend by now. The warmth and richness of it roll across my skin, and I'm immediately covered in goosebumps. No, he sure doesn't look like his pictures. He's actually much, much hotter. The features are similar, and for a moment I wonder if I've gone loopy or if... I don't know what... I put the thought to the side. For me, his looks are an upgrade. I just hope he's not disappointed in my appearance...I just have to calm

down. I feel like I sound too excited. I inhale and exhale, and I feel my breasts rise and fall self-consciously. I'm wearing a white tank shirt with thin spaghetti straps and a loose, flowy orange wrapper on top of it hiding some of my heft, a blue girly skirt with a flare and floral print designs and black ballet flats.Jennifer said sometimes men exaggerate their height so she noted that you should always take off 2 inches from whatever they say. And for women you should always add 30 pounds to whatever they say, she said as well, which made me laugh. I didn't mention my bit of extra weight, but I hoped that the pictures would be as honest as they were flattering. He is a vision. He said he was 6 foot 4. He is a towering 6'4"....Which is wonderful to my 5 foot 9, making me feel small and feminine. I look up at him. I'm sitting, and when I stand to shake his hand, I am still looking up, dirty blonde hair slightly shaggy tousled as though he just went through the day in the wind and Sun. he is wearing a soft gray vee neck shirt and blue jeans that were well worn and rest lovingly on his hips. To say that he is athletic would be an understatement. To me, I could only think the words "Greek god." His frame is entirely muscular with firm pectorals and abs that you could probably grate cheese on. Oops… He sees me perusing him. I glance up from my ogling, and he smiles. It's a beautiful bright toothpaste commercial smile. I laugh nervously.
"So. How are you doing?" He says laughing, trying to break the ice. He reaches for my extended hand and pulls me into a hug. I can't help but feel enveloped in warmth and peace. He smells like Christmas, like pine needles and cinnamon and a crackling fireplace. The hug seems to be morphing into more of an embrace now. My nipples perk from the pressure from

his broad chest. Wait, is he smelling my hair? I'm sure I'm bright red right now with the blush from his open acknowledgment of my ogling.

"Sorry. I told you I'm nervous."

"That's alright. Am I acceptable?" he teases, but I feel as though he is also nervous too. His stance is off as if he is used to the ogling and I'm not sure I like that. When a guy is this pretty, I'm sure he thinks he can have whatever he wants. I poke him.

"Now, you know that there is no one on this God's green earth that would not think that you are acceptable, Greg. You know that." I huff. "You're a very good-looking man, and now you're just playing with me." Looking directly into his blue eyes, I'm daring him. "I suggest you don't." He stares at me silently for a moment looking into my eyes. They seem to acknowledge... Something. And I feel as though they approve. Of what? My sass, my petulant mouth?

"Yes. I do get a lot of looks. But not for the reason you think." He gestures to the tiny banquette that I have commandeered.

"You mean girls aren't looking at you because you're so physically appealing? I find that hard to believe!" As we sit, I am struck again by how tall he is. I feel light-hearted and embarrassed at the same time. He is looking at me again, thoughtfully, as if he wanted to say something but decided against it. He nibbles his lower lip. I find this motion endearing and childlike. He takes my hand and holds it, leaning in and in a low almost whisper he asks,

"Are we going to talk about how I look all night Kaitlin because I would like to discuss you. "

"Okay." I gulp. "What would you like to know?" He is playing with my hand now, examining the nails, turning it over and

caressing my palm. "Wait where are my manners?" I hop up. " can I get you a coffee, Greg?" I stand and breathe deeply, thankful from my brief respite of all this instant chemistry. "I'll get it, but thanks, but can I get you another?" He says eying my now almost empty coffee. "Thank you. Cafe Americano please."
"Anything in it?" Boy, he's is so happy and energetic, it reminds me of a puppy.
"Sugar-free vanilla and 2 spend, oh and cream. Thank you." As he walks up to the counter, I cannot help but watch his well-formed backside as he casually strolls up and orders. The barista eyes him with big moon eyes as if he's some sort of movie star. His mega-watt smile has done her in as well. A few minutes later, as he sits down across from me again and hands me my coffee, our hands just barely brush, and I feel a jolt of electricity straight to my miss kitty. I look up and see that it seems he felt something too. I let the thought sit in my head for a moment before dismissing it, allowing a moment to dream before the blowup that I am sure is to follow. Yes, I'm meeting him, but I know myself well enough to know this will not go past tonight. So instead, I feel the warmth of my coffee and try to revel in the feeling of this moment in time.
"Mmm, it's good. Thank you." Greg and me? My dirty mind wanders. What would that be like?
"Well first off, I want to say that you do look lovely and I was trying to be a gentleman and not ogle your beautiful breasts." He leans in a little too close and continues softly near my ear. "I also want to bite your lovely lips, but we're not there yet." I inhale sharply, feeling his breath very close to the delicate shell of my ear, picturing him doing exactly what he said. I quickly laugh it off, as I look down and see the baristas phone

number with "call me" written on my coffee cup... I turn it, grinning so that Greg can see.

"See! I'm not the only one..." We both laugh and the tension dissipates. I can't help but think... I know why I'm single. Now, I have to wonder why this not just handsome, but an outright gorgeous man who I've just witnessed has women falling all over him, is supposedly alone.

"Why are you single?" I blurt out, while I have the courage."I know why I am, but you... You are a beautiful guy, Greg. You have a good job." I state sincerely, trying to soften the question. "You seem, I know you hate to hear it, but genuinely nice. And I've just witnessed the barista throw herself at you... Which I'm sure happens all the time. Don't get me wrong... I'm glad I am able to hang out with you today, but why are we here?" I gesture my hands between us. He sips his coffee thoughtfully for a full minute and looks at me in what I can only assume is a power move used in big board rooms. A long moment passes before he speaks again.

"Well... a solid tan finger lightly strokes his lower lips as he contemplates. "Let me answer your question with a question. Because, Kaitlin, I know why I'm here, but I want to know now why are you're here? When we began speaking, it was you who reached out to me. Why? And when we texted with each other why did you continue to do so? And when I asked you to meet me today why did you agree?" With every word he is leaning closer and closer to me and warmth floods me in a kind of scary, exciting way. My blood is pounding in my ears. "Kaitlin?" I can smell his winter minty breath. He is so close now, that if I were to tilt my head, we would be kissing.

"Because! Of all the reasons I just said.!" It comes out as an almost exhausted whisper, low and gravelly. "Because I can see myself cuddling with you on the couch after a long day at work. Because you seem like the kind of guy who I would really like to... be with." I say this all in one small breath, feeling exposed. He reaches down and grabs my hands again, and looks into my eyes. Picking up my hands, he gently kisses them, smiling. "Those reasons you said, Kaitlin. All those reasons, that's why." He smirks at me and I feel so connected to him at this moment. Outside of our little bubble, a baby begins to wail, pulling us from our little moment. The Coffee Shop is starting to get a little full of people, and I feel as though they are looking at us. I feel raw inside as if I'd been scrubbed.

"Hey." He pulls me from my darker thoughts, pinching my hand. "Do you want to get out of here?" He suggests, sensing my discomfort."I don't live too far away, and I promise I'll behave. Maybe we can do just that. Sit on the couch after a long day at work and hang out?" He has used my own words against me. I smile to myself. Well, why not ride this thing, whatever it is, till the wheels fall off.

"I would really like that."

He takes my hand as we walk out of the Coffee Shop. When we're in the parking lot he asks, "Where are you parked at?"
"Oh, I took an Uber here."
"Okay, well I have a driver today so..." He says almost embarrassed. "Shall we?"
I inhale deeply feeling as if I'm blushing head to toe. He wraps his arm around my shoulders, and we walk toward a black town car.
"Is this the Uber black?"

"Something like that." He opens the door for me into a beautifully appointed town car. The smell of recently polished leather seats is almost decadent. Cool air engulfs my senses as I slide across the smooth seat allowing him to enter the same door that I entered. Once secure and belted he says to the driver,
"Home please, Hawk."
"Yes, Sir." The car heads toward the hills of Hollywood and beyond...

Chapter Three

He reaches out and grabs my hand. His hands are warm and soft. He turns my palm up and traces designs into it as we ride along in companionable silence. He looks at me. I look back in wonder. I'm having a wonderful time even though we really haven't exchanged too many words , in person at least. We talked forever on the phone. Maybe that's it. We learned so much about each other when we talked on the phone, that we're old friends now. Really deep down I feel a tiny particle of hope that this might be a real connection. My past experience would beg to differ, so I take it as is appears. That I'm a really lucky girl. I am making a promise to myself, here and now, to have as much fun as possible tonight, with the full knowledge that there may well not be a night number two.
"Would you like to hear some music?" Between the curlicue pattern he is drawing on my hands, and his whole energy, I feel almost drugged, I am so relaxed.
"Yeah okay." He pushes a button, and smooth jazz encompasses our senses. I feel oddly comfortable in his company. He stares out the window, smiling thinking to himself, happy, drawing curlicue patterns on my palm. I can't understand why I feel so comfortable with this man. I feel as though this new car smell is working like aromatherapy and I really feel very light, especially after such a long day at work. I look up for my musings feeling his gaze.
"Penny for your thoughts?"
"I can't help but think I feel very relaxed around you."
"Me too. Which is really odd for me." The way he bites his lush lower lip every now and then, makes me think he's experiencing the same sense of awe as I am. "Is it the same

for you? Are you normally relaxed around people you just met?"

"Not all!" I laugh easily thinking of my youth." I'm kinda person to put on my party face in public, but it's not real. In truth, I feel like a homebody. I want to get out more, but I feel more comfortable enjoying the quiet evening at home. When I was younger, I wanted to go out dancing with my friends." I pause, in a true moment of introspection. "Or, I guess I thought I did. When I think back, I wanted to be with my friends, and they wanted to go out dancing. Is that terrible?" I ask, shocked by my own revelation.

"Not all. I'm a homebody as well. My work has me out on the town for social occasions dressed like a monkey in suits. But I'd rather have jeans or sweats on, hiking or doing something physical."

"I noticed that in your profile." I hesitate to bring up anything negative. But still. "You have a lot of physical pictures." I pause for a moment thinking about my catfish worries. "I worry a bit because I'm not that physical a person."

"Don't be worried." he lifts my hand and places a lingering kiss on my pulse point, his lips resting a moment too long, yet somehow not long enough. The sensation curls my toes.

"We have arrived." The driver, Hawk, murmurs. I look out the window and see we have climbed the hills to a... palace retreat, maybe? It's big and beautiful and sleek. But it also seems calming and natural. Lots of sleek windows and large rooms visible before we reach the courtyard. It's grounds are surrounded by smooth stones and three koi ponds.

"Ready?"

I nod, speechless. When he said he worked at a bank, I guess I thought he was a bank manager. This makes me even more sure this will end badly. I make very little as a dressmaker's assistant. Don't get me wrong. I absolutely love what I do, creating wearable art. Mrs. Jensen has even taken some of my designs and added them to her lines, giving me a bonus, when she does.

"The bank is doing well for you, I take it?"

Greg laughs shyly, almost as though he is insecure about bringing me here. "It's just money, Angel."

"I thought you were a banker."

"I am a banker. I just happen to be excellent at my job."

"Believe me. I don't care." I laugh. "I have every intention of using you for your body." I can tell the topic of money makes him nervous, so I change the subject. "So, do I get to meet the puppy and kitties??? I miss having pets. I can't wait!"

"Absolutely! Right now if you want!" He grins ear to ear, happy for the reprieve. Reaching into his pocket he pulls out a remote that does not only unlock but also opens the door. He whistles loudly and yells,

"Honey, I'm home!" I hear it before I see it. The clattering of paws running across the floor, and suddenly a beautiful, energetic, one-year-old Rottweiler barrels towards us. She skitters to a halt, actually running into Greg, bowling him slightly into me. She is big, 90 pounds big, and her black coat shines brightly. And as big as she is, she excited to see her daddy!

"Hey, honey!" He kneels down scratching her with affection. I bend down to join him turning my palm backward so that Honey can take in my scent first. She smells me first, then nudges my hand and licks it. As I scratch her, I notice her scars, clipped ears, and tail, telling the story of the sad life she had led before Greg got her from the shelter. She leans her head into my palm, for more contact, bowling me over a bit.

"She's beautiful!" I smile, happy I have her stamp of approval. "I'm so glad you were able to rescue her. Rottweilers get such a bad rep."

"It looks like you know about dogs. I think when we talked on the phone you said you used to have a Rottweiler. Is that right?" He is grinning big now.

"When I was younger. His name was Dawg."

"Your dog's name was Dog?" He laughs.

"No. Dawg. D a w g. He was such a gentle soul too. Rottweiler. I don't think there are bad dogs, but just wrong people." I murmur, stroking Honey's coat.

"I like that... Come on...movie?" He stands up, dusting off his hands and reaches out for mine. I gently place my hand in his and follow him in.

The living room is such an open, inviting space. It's filled with decadent wood, plush furnishings, and lots of wall length windows. But the focal point is a massive fireplace built with jutting rocks creating a cascading waterfall flowing down the rocks in quiet beauty.

"So? Movie?"

"Can we get a drink first? Do you mind?"

"Oh! I'm sorry! Where my manners. ? What would you like to drink?"

"I love a glass of wine or rum you have it?"

"I have both. What would you prefer? "

"Let me ask you. What do you like to drink Greg?" He looks surprised as if no-one has ever actually asked him what he likes.I know I'm wrong, but he seems very thoughtful, as if I'm some sort of novelty. I don't know how that makes me feel. I pray to God he is not putting me into the sister/friends box. He has me at his house. He is gorgeous, sweet and thoughtful. Not that I wouldn't mind being his friend not that I wouldn't mind being his friend. But just staring at his full lush smiling lips, makes me think of kissing him...
"I like a nice red. I do also enjoy a good rum, or an Irish whiskey or scotch ,but I have to be the mood for that. How about a nice Malbec?"
"Perfect! " He seems to think I'm nervous. Maybe he's nervous. I get the impression that he's worried about his wealth. Little does he know I'm not taking this date very seriously. Yeah, so he has money. I don't really care. Not that I think it would make a difference in the long run but I know my self-worth. that is I know the value of my appearance and demeanor in the open market. I'm a 4 and this man standing before me is a solid 9. I wouldn't go so far just say he was a 10 he has the cutest little scar on his chin and his timidness is a slight turn off at times. Maybe I need to take things into my own hands. Could I, though? Could I be so brave? As we walk through to the kitchen, I feel a chill and feel the hairs on my arms stands on end.
"Cold?"
"Just a slight chill" He's very observant. He holds up a finger meaning wait, and sprints, a man on a mission. He returns a moment later with an Afghan. I am immediately warmed not only by the blanket but also the gesture. As he comes up behind me to drape it over my shoulders, he comes in close.

Very close. I feel the warmth of his breath on the sensitive skin at my nape and almost swoon at the feeling as his full front contacts with my whole backside. I think I even feel his erection nudging me. I hear a moan, and I can't tell if it was him or me. I hope it was him. I can't think how embarrassed I would be if it is me.

"Thank you." I say in an almost whisper... I look over my left shoulder while still wrapped in my blanket of Afghan to Greg and up into the pools of the ocean blue that are his eyes. Our faces are so close... Kiss me.... Kiss me... I try to will him with my mind. Almost sadly he pulls away, me unkissed, and heads to collect our drinks. He has a wine cabinet that's well stocked and forages for a moment for the right bottle, making quick work of it. In sampling his selection, I nearly melt with pleasure. It's beautiful. Very berry with notes of spice and vanilla. I know it's me that moans this time. In sheer appreciation as I warm and relax rolling the malbec in my mouth. We settle in the den, another warm and comforting, but also richly decadent room. It's all notes of dark rich woods and soft leather furnishings. He puts on a scary movie that's also got a little comedy in it. I have never seen a tv this big before. Not that either of us is paying attention. Soon after we settled into our cuddling position, Honey and 2 beautiful calico kittens, Cinnamon and Charlie, bounce into our laps. In my one hand, I have my wine, which I rest on Greg's knee. In the other, I am idly stroking the kitty and puppies fur. Greg is leisurely stroking the nape of my neck. I know it's too soon, really, but I feel so relaxed and content in this moment. Oh, sure, there are a million thoughts floating through my head, tugging on my insecurities. Like how the nape of my neck is not very feminine. And I'm sure he can feel my love handles pushed against him as I snuggle close, but it feels so damn good to be held like this. I steel myself and decide that I am definitely going to squeeze every last drop out of this evening and commit it to memory for the next dry spell sure to come. I feel the heat of his stare and look up to see his face very close to mine. His skin is flushed and his eyes seem lazy and half hooded. Almost like lust.He bends very, very slowly, and our lips meet. The kiss is almost a whisper, it's so soft. He dips in again, lingering this time. Soft, pliant nibbling lips sending a corresponding tug straight to my womb. My breasts feel heavy, and my clit throbs. I feel like a teenage boy. Like I'm in my sexual peak. I've have never thought of myself as a good kisser, but the way Greg kisses me feels better than any of the sex I have had. I moan low and give myself into the kiss urging him on.

He pulls away abruptly.
"More wine!" His exclamation is breathless and a little too loud, as he jumps, separating himself from me. I feel like he's trying to put some distance between us. I wonder if my blatant desire has somehow scared him off. Yes, my glass is empty, but it has been for a while now. It wasn't until I clung to him in that kiss, that he jumped. Though, when he returns a few minutes later, he seems calmer. Whoa, what is that!? As he hands me the wine, my gaze is stuck on the fact that he has a massive and thoroughly impressive erection. Maybe that's why he jumped.He's worried that I had felt his goodies. The movie is winding down now. I worry that he is trying to cool things down. Maybe he thinks I have the wrong idea. We have returned to a similarly cuddly position, but it is evident

his guard is up. He turns to meet my gaze before giving my shoulders an abrupt squeeze and a bird peck of a kiss on the forehead. The forehead! I try and think quickly. I grab my glass tipping it backing and making easy work of the fruity liquid courage, hoping it will be enough to make me bold. "What did you think?" He yawns, smiling and seems relaxed. I need to take matters into my own hands. Literally.
"Honestly?" I tilt my head, hoping to challenge him.
"Always."
Deep breath.
"I could hardly watch it with any sort of focus, with your strong hands working their magic on my neck" I stand and slowing peel off the orange wrapper from my shoulders slowly. As it glides down my body to the floor,I reach out my hand holding it out for him to join me. He smiles up at me, quite innocently. He has no idea what's rolling around in my head. I make my stand and let the chips fall. When he stands, after I have tugged his hands a few times mind you, I pull him in close and place a whisper of a wet kiss on his neck. My hand slowly slides down his athletic torso and glides over, quite purposefully, his jean clad cock. When he inhales sharply, I tiptoe, reaching for his mouth, pressing my lips firmly and using my tongue to gently lick him.
"Hey," I whisper breathlessly against his neck. "Show me your room." My hand is still fully pressing against his growing erection. Hopefully, there can be no mistake as to my intentions.
"You don't really want to see my room, Kaitlin." His breath is hoarse and gravelly.
"Yes, Greg. I really. Really. Really do." I say each word between lush kisses.

"No. You don't. You want a beautiful calm evening and a kiss at your doorstep." reaching up, he runs his fingers through my hair, molding them to the shape of my scalp. "Remember, Angel. It took three phone dates just to get us here. Which is meeting face to face for the first time at a Coffee Shop, by the way. I like you a lot, and it's getting late." He gently takes my hand off of him and kisses it to soften the rejection. When he steps back, I push him back down onto the couch. It's quite a shove, with him being so big and solid.

"Look at me." I stare up. His eyes are wired, sparkling blue bolts. He's turned on, but also unsure. It feels to me like he is the kind of guy who always likes to be in control. Like he's laughing at me trying to boss him. Still, I'm so glad he's big. It's a rare thing for me to feel small and weaker than anyone. His hands are on my hips now, firm against my now sensitive skin. He is looking at me sternly, but he's also nibbling his bottom lip. I've gathered by now that's his worry tell.

I grab two handfuls of his shirt, pulling him flush against me. "No. You heard right. I said look at me, Boss Man. Time to get real. The picture you sent me in your profile wasn't you." I pause to gauge his reaction. "I feel like I know you, Greg. But I don't know who you are." I push him back down, straddling him, I leaned in close and whisper into his ear, gently nipping it. "Guess what, though? My nails graze his scalp. "I don't care. You're a nice guy. That's all that matters." I grab his chin for emphasis. "Yeah. you've got money. I don't care. I don't make a lot at all. Do you care? We don't know if there's going to be a tomorrow or next time. Do we?" I pause again, looking into his eyes for emphasis. "One hundred percent of my relationships have ended." I kiss him gently now. "I bet your batting average is currently the same. Now take my hand." I peck his lips quickly and stand, my breath a little shaky. "and show me your room now." I put emphasis on the now.

"Yes, Ma'am..."

Up the winding stairs we go, stopping by the kitchen for the wine bottle. His bedroom is like heaven. It's such an open space, comfortable, lived in, and dominated by a huge bed. When we cross the threshold, though, the energy changes. Greg has turned into something else entirely. Very alpha. I can feel my body responding. Even his stride, his breathing is different.

"Now." He smiles at me. He grabs the back of my head and pulls my head back to look up at him. "You look at me." He is walking me backward toward the bed. He never breaks the amazing eye contact. "You are very smart, Kaitlin. That's one of the many things I like about you. We are gonna have a good long talk. But not right now. Right now, we are in my bedroom. And in this room, I'm in charge." His hands tighten in my hair, pulling my head back to an awkward angle, exposing my rapidly beating pulse. "You couldn't wait. You wanted it now, huh? "I blink up at him, having stumbled now onto the bed. Mr. Shy and unsure is gone and has been replaced by a super alpha. Kinda hot. But also kinda not. This isn't the real him. I've seen the lip nibbling geek that's locked in those baby blues, and I don't want to settle for less. Especially if this is the only time.

"No."

He releases my hair and steps back, confused. I guess that is not the usual answer he gets. I take a step forward, then another. Placing my hand flat on his chest and slowly walking forward, forcing him to walk backward.

"You forget, Greg. We, and I mean we, Greg, have had three phone dates, really more like 4. You and I have talked more than any relationship I've ever had. We did talk till one in the morning. So I know the last thing you really want is to put on the macho ,"I'm in charge" hat on. I spin, pulling him down on the bed with me and flip again to where I'm on top. And I hate being on top. The wine must be making me bold. "Now correct me if I'm wrong. You're a nine."

"I'm a nine?" He laughs, smirking.

"You're. A. Nine." I poke his chest to confirm each word. "And as a nine, I'm sure there have been certain expectations. The kind where you get whatever you want. Well, I'm a four, buddy. And where I come from we gotta get while the getting is good. And if the getting ain't good, I gotta get gone." I'm sure I'm blushing beet red when that crazy sentence leaves my mouth.

I'm straddling his chest now, and we are both laughing. It feels comfortable again. His hands come up, and he rubs my lower lips with the pad of his thumb. My pussy is flush against his long, still clothed shaft and a jolt of pleasure silences me. "Seriously…" I lean down, gently running my lips along his jaw. "Let's have fun. And several orgasms." I roll over pulling him back on top. "Now pour me a drink, Mr. Put on some music, so I can get out of my own head. And then," I grin slowly, wagging my brows." I want you to strip for me. Now." I put a little extra force into my voice, when he moves slowly. I have never in my life been so bold. But I really do feel comfortable. And he deserves it after that 'I'm in charge' line.

Also the fact that I can't plan on seeing him after tonight is keeping me from worrying about how I'll be seen.

"Yes, Ma'am."

As he heads downstairs for the glasses we forgot, I lower the lights hoping it will help me to be less self-conscious. He returns, noticing the change and turns them back up. Just a little. I'm sure he knew why I did it. He hands me a new glass of white wine. I tentatively take a sip. It's a crisp sauvignon blanc. I grin at his ability to do just the right thing. It's chilled and fresh and calming. He sets the music to a light wordless jazz station on Pandora, and then he slowly begins to strip. First the soft t-shirt. Slowly gliding up revealing taut abs and a sparse happy trail. Hard pectoral muscles follow. And his biceps dance as he whips it over his head and tosses it at my face. I laugh and smell the shirt in a way that I hope seems pervy, trying to be funny.

 "Slower baby," I say, hoping I sound sexy.

"Yes, Daddy." His voice is trying for falsetto. He's playing along. Good. He does a little twirl. When he is facing away from me, he looks over his shoulder being coy, sticking out his butt. While staring at me, he unzips his pants in what could only be called a very convincing girl stripper routine. He shimmies out of the jeans revealing corded thigh muscles and lightly furred calves. Now all he is wearing are tight black boxer briefs. He's walking towards me with a deceptively casual grace. When he reaches me, he pounces. He is above me now, with his hands pinning my own above my head. His eyes are shining brightly, and his smile is genuine and whole. I'm probably reflecting the same in my eyes. I shudder as his fingertips slowing peel up my shirt over my belly and over my chest only to stop when it reaches my face, blocking my view, but revealing my nose and chin and mouth, which he immediately takes advantage, kissing me deeply. I feel consumed as his tongue whirls around, dancing with my own. Each tug as he sucks on my lips sends a matching pull in my core. Wet Kisses trail a path down the side of my neck. When he reaches my breasts, he slows. I can't see, but I feel like he's staring at me. I try to imagine what I must look like, all flush, hopefully not too sweaty, chest heaving with excitement. I try to not think of the ampleness of my flesh. And now I am thinking of nothing as his wet mouth slowly covers my right nipple through the bra. I know it's me that moans as I suppress the urge to wiggle and thrash. The sensation is so intense. When I bite my lip to quiet myself, both cups of the bra are jerked down.

"No, Katy baby, I want to hear your pleasure. Talk to me." He releases my hands, only long enough to remove my bra. Then he uses my shirt to secure my hands together. I'm a little nervous. I've never been restrained during sex before. "I'll try." And I will . Tonight is my night to be brave. And now that I have my sight back, my eyes feast on the sight of Greg hovering over me. His hands roam over my skin, my arms, the sides of my breasts, my belly. Soft, feather-light caresses, barely there but the effect is like a slap to miss kitty. He looks right at me as his head dips down to suckle and lick at my nipples. He lavishes a great deal of attention there. I'm watching him as he is looking at me. It is one of the hottest things I have ever experienced.

I'm breathing very roughly now as he gives me kisses on his way down my belly, stopping every now and again the suck and nibble on various places. His tongue licks into my belly button, and my body coils with the intense pleasure of it. His hands are sliding down the sides of my waist and as he reaches my blue girly skirt, his finger slips under the end and begins pushing my skirt and my panties down slowly. I can feel the impact as it slides down past my knees and calves and feel the pressure of his fingertips against my heels as it slides off of me completely. A rush of cold air hits my hot skin. The sensation is overwhelming. I feel almost ticklish as he nibbles his way back up my legs quickly. He pauses only at the backs of my thighs, and then journeys on until he reaches my center. I feel his hot breath on me right before he kisses the top of my mound.

"You smell so good," he whispers into my pussy. Then I feel his nose nuzzling my clit. I have to force myself to keep my legs open. I want this, but I'm also embarrassed. And there is just something about his voice that has me dripping. I can actually feel the sensation sliding slowly down my cheeks.

"You like this?" He smiles as he parts my folds and takes a long lick from bottom to clit, my body feeling every millimeter of his wide tongue. I jerk, every muscle in me responding to his expert touch.

"Relax." He coos against my folds. My whole body is shaking with tension, yet he is just leisurely lapping like a kitten in cream. Lap, lap, lap. In and up and playfully suckling my clit every so often. It feels wonderful, but it's not building to release. So I grab his head by the hair and try to gently pull him up to me, hinting that maybe it is more effort than it's worth down there.

"Relax." He says again.

"I'm trying. But I don't want your jaw to fall off down there."

"I love it down here. I could live down here, hearing those little sounds in the back of your throat when you like a touch. It's so good. Does it feel good?" Which is a silly question, because he just said he can tell when I like a particular touch. "You know I like it... I'm just not close is all. I want this to be fun for both of us."

"I wasn't trying to make you come, Baby. I was just getting you warmed up. Now if you'll excuse me..." I can taste my own essence as he leans up and kisses me deeply before heading south again. Boy, howdy he is thorough! Licking and sucking and nibbling on my folds... I embrace it and let go, becoming quite vocal at all of the new sensations. His hands had been massaging my thighs, but now they are coming closer... One Solid, long finger enters me and strokes upward, finding the right spot, the magic spot that causes my whole body to attempt curling into a ball. Whoa! I can feel the vibration as he laughs into my pussy. He knows what he's doing. I'll give him that. When I finally am adjusted to the sensation of him strumming the delicate flesh inside me, he adds another finger and strokes even firmer . The feeling triples and my toes curl. Sharp shooting spasms of pleasure... I'm mewling and grabbing his head again, not to escape now, but to pull him closer. I can't help it. I feel like I'm falling. Then the playful licking stops and his hands still inside of me. The change is abrupt. Cold air assaults me as he blows on my little button, now not so little now, but filled and throbbing with the beat of my excited heart.

"Come for me baby. I want to hear your pleasure." And just quickly as it stopped, my almost there orgasm shoots to the surface as his lips latch onto my clit and suck, hard and deep, while the two fingers plunge anew curling quickly and rhythmically onto that magic, wonderful spot. My orgasm is long and loud and violent and glorious. He keeps the pressure perfectly in place and slows and gentles as I float down from heaven. Now he's laughing and breathing heavily on my mound. I really think he enjoyed that, giving me pleasure. He kisses my core once more before kissing his way back up my body. I am still breathless when he kisses me again deeply, and I am so turned, on tasting myself on his tongue.

"That was beautiful, Kaitlin. I love how honest you are with your pleasure." He's looking at me now, gazing into my eyes. "Wine?" He nibbles at my chin, to lighten and break this intense connection. I nod, still breathless and trembling. That has to be the most intense orgasm I have ever had. Not that I'll tell him that. I'm quite sure he'd get a big head. Also, if that is par for the course, I'm sure he's been told plenty of times.

I sip with passion. The sauvignon blanc is perfect. If I were to purposely create wine for during sex, this would be it. the cold, crisp Rush of grapefruit relaxes me, and I wrap myself in a sheet and sip, allowing the refreshing liquid to bring me back down. Greg nuzzles up to me spooning me and takes the glass from my hand and drinks deeply. I commit this to memory as the perfect moment. He refills the glass, takes a large mouthful, then another, transferring the wine from his mouth to mine.

"You know…" I laugh, slightly recovered now. "The Olympics, the first performance is always given an eight point five setting the bar for everything that comes after it," I say jokingly.

"What are you saying?" He grins. "That you won't expect anything less now? That was my plan." Smiling, he wags his eyebrows.

"No... What I meant was, get ready for me to show you what a nine looks like buddy! "I pounce on top of him playfully, feeling energized. I take his hands and press them to my breasts kneading myself using him. I reach for his hair and arch his head back while kissing all over his face, neck, and nibbling his ears. Sliding my nails gently down his torso, I find his small brown male nipples and lavish them with attention as though he were a girl. Kissing my way down his belly, I plunge my tongue in the button simulating an act soon to come. And now I am here at the promise land. I pause for a moment admiring his tight black boxer briefs. I put my face right there, inhaling his scent fully through the fabric.

"Hips please," I say with the edge of the fabric in my teeth. When he lifts , I slowly take the material down an inch at a time opening it like a cherished present. I don't look up at him yet, as I want to keep my courage. And I need it. His cock is big and beautiful, long and straight. Not too big, like a monster, though, but more like a solid nine inches, thick and heavy. I'm straight up staring now. In the back of my mind, I wonder what is wrong with him. He seems perfect. I'll figure it out soon enough, I'm sure. For now, I'm just going to enjoy the ride. And I do mean ride.

"See something you like?" Guess I have been caught.

"Just thinking what I should call him..." I grin biting my lip thoughtfully. "He looks like a gentleman warrior. Do you call him anything?"

"Do I? No. But he's been called names. Actually, he's a bit sensitive."

"I should hope so. Sensitivity should make my job easy. I think I shall call him Apollo. " I say thoughtfully kissing the head. "God of the sun, music, healing. Is that ok?"

"I like it" He is biting his lip, and leaning back on his forearms watching me intently.

I open my mouth as wide as I can and sink down on his shaft. I feel full of light-hearted playfulness. When he is as deep as I can comfortably take him, I push just a little further and swallow. I want him to feel me deeply. I begin the rhythmic up and down along his cock, licking softly at the tip, and suckling deeply at the base, basically teasing him. I look up at him, licking my palm, before returning to my ministrations, while adding my hand to fondle him. He is looking down on me, stroking my hair lightly. I love that he is encouraging me, but not forcing me. His soft murmurs of appreciating my work grow more frantic and are making my pussy clench in wanting to be filled. Clearly, he is close. Wanting to feel him inside me when he explodes, yet wanting the power of making him writhe, I reluctantly slow. I look up slowly after one long last lick.

"Condom." I sound breathless, even to my own ears.

"Nightstand." I'm so glad he sounds desperate as well, that I'm not alone in this. I reach up and find not only condoms, but also scented lube, unopened, thank God. I grab one and gingerly open it rolling it onto his beautiful shaft.

I am flipped, and I'm suddenly on my back staring up at a grinning Greg.

"You are so. Fucking. Beautiful." He breathes as he leans in for a kiss. This kiss, is different. It is soft, and tender. He laps gently at my lips before delving inside and caressing my tongue in a worshipping manner. I close my eyes , feeling overwhelmed with emotions that I can't explain. I grab his head and run my fingers through his hair pulling him closer feeling like it is too much and yet, I can't get enough. His hand is reaching down now, touching my core, feeling just how slippery and ready I am. His cock rests across my folds now, lazily slipping across, just barely brushing my clit. He's waiting for something. What? I open my eyes to see him staring back at me. His ocean blue gaze is penetrating my innermost being, and I am overwhelmed. It is only now that he sees me seeing him, that he leans down to kiss me and thrusts. It's a long smooth stroke and my breath catches.I know with great certainty that I have never experienced anything like this before. No gentle, tentative nudging, but, instead, long powerful strokes. As he begins to catch his rhythm, I feel a glorious, languid sensation wash over me. My eyes start to flutter closed, but I am jerked sharply back into the moment, as he grabs a handful of my hair, arching my neck.

"Look at me, Kaitlin. Know that it's me giving this pleasure to you. Show me with your eyes what you're feeling." His thrusts punctuate each sentence. I'm floating now. The feeling is too intense, too sharp, too powerful.

"Give it to me Katy baby. Let me see you shatter."

With that, his hand reaches down and presses firmly on my clit. Intense electric bursts of pleasure rip through me, shattering me. I cry out his name as the most powerful orgasm I have ever known moves through me, radiating through my entire body. It goes on and on. And on, and on. I am frantically chanting his name now, my mind completely lost. Greg's thrusts have become more erratic now, shorter and jerky. Coming down from my high now, slightly, I suddenly want him to feel what I'm feeling. I reach up, cupping his cheeks with my hands. I grab a fistful of his hair

pulling his head back, letting him feel our urgency. I clench my muscles deep inside, smiling up at him.
"Now you show me. Show me that you're here with me too. Give me something to remember." I pull his head down to mine and kiss him deeply pressing my tongue into his mouth, thrusting. With that, I can feel him shatter entirely. He moans into my mouth as he jerks and spasms. After what seems like an eternity of his warmth surrounding me, and his full weight acting like the best blanket ever, his head lifts from the crook of my neck. He looks up at me with a sheepish grin.
"Hey."
"Hey."

We lay here for minutes. Just staring at each other. His hand slowly creating designs on my arm. It's an incredible sensation, but I know that real life is going to interrupt soon enough. I'm just debating if we have time for another round of pleasure before the awkwardness begins.
As if he can read my mind he leans over and kisses me.

Chapter Four

I am having so much trouble focusing on work today. Right now, I've been trying to cut this dress pattern for what seems like an eternity. Times today, as I smoothed my hands down the fabric to smooth it, I remembered the soft sensation of Greg's hands gliding down my body. I'm basically staring at this blue satin, thinking about his eyes. I mean his eyes aren't naturally this shade, but when he was doing things to me last night, awesome, hot things, there were times, when his eyes would darken to this gorgeous shade of midnight blue. Like when he looked up at me as he kissed his way down my belly…

"Are you ok?"
My coworker, Josh touches my shoulder, and I am pulled, momentarily from daydreaming.
"You look distracted, Babe. You need a break?"
"I'm fine. Just daydreaming, I guess." I'm sure I'm beet red. If anyone knew where my mind has been today, I would explode.
"What about?" He is really close now, perching his elbows on my workstation.
"Nothing really. I was reading a good book last night, and it is stuck in my head." There's no way I'm gonna tell the truth here.
"Well, it must have been really good, because you're glowing Katy girl." Am I glowing? Well, it has been a long time since I have had that much fun. On the date, or otherwise, really. I

know Greg, and I have been talking for a while on the phone, and I really feel like I got to know him in those conversations that we had. I guess that's kind of why I decided to meet him. Thinking back on last night, I feel kind of bad about sneaking out in the middle of the night like I did. But I believe that it's better to end on a high note. We really didn't have that much in common. And there is a lot I don't really know about Greg. I mean, I know he's got money, which I don't really care about, but he seems to be really uncomfortable about it. And also, after what I went through with my ex, Daniel, I'm not in any place to put myself out there again. So for sure, I'm hoping to preserve last night as a beautiful little bubble of perfection. The perfect night. My womb clenches firmly, an aftershock, a glorious reminder of all that happened last night.

"Hello, earth to Katy. Wow." Josh is waving his hands in front of my face and smiling now. "It must have been a really good book. You are out of it today. Mrs. Jenson will be in soon." he subtly reminds me of my deadline.

"I guess I should hurry up then." He touches my arm briskly and heads off, back to the counter in the front of the shop.

He's so sweet. I must really be out of it, if Josh, who doesn't generally notice me at all sees a difference.

Tonight I'm definitely going to bake some thank you muffins for Jennifer. That app is the best thing that has happened to me in… ever.

I have finally finished this blue dress's pattern, when a young, clean cut gentleman carrying a huge bouquet of red and pink roses, gingerly walks into the workshop. "Kaitlin McEntire?"

I can't help myself. I know I'm practically vibrating with excitement. I raise my hand.

"Sign here please." I quickly scribble my signature.

"Wait one moment, please. I need to grab my bag to tip you."
"Not necessary Ma'am. That has already been taken care of." He dips his head in salute, and quickly exits.
Both Jennifer and Josh seem to have appeared out of nowhere. Jennifer is bouncing, excited. She pushes me aside, rather violently, and opens the card. She slumps sadly, then begins bouncing all over again.
"They're for Kaitlin!" I guess she thought they were for her, which really makes more sense if I think about it. I mean these are the first flowers I have ever received. That thought kind of makes me sad.
"Ahem." She adopts her story teller voice. "It reads, 'I had a great time last night. You left without saying goodbye. Can't wait for you to call me. Greg.' Oooh! Who's Greg?" her blonde hair is practically a halo around her, she's bouncing so much.
"Intrigue! Magic app?"
I push past Josh who is hovering over her shoulder and grab the card. Hmm. "Can't wait for you to call me." Silently smiling, I take the flowers to my little box of an office. I really ought to call, to say thank you for the flowers at least.

I sit for a minute and just breathe. I feel as if every cell of my body is electrified. I guess good sex will do that to you. My nipples are tender, and my whole sex is swollen and every step I have taken today has reminded me of his skills in bed. Taking a deep breath, I reach for the phone just as it rings.
"Mrs. Jensen's Custom Boutique. Kaitlin speaking. How can I help you?"
"Hi." Greg's warm honeyed voice assaults me.
"Hi?" I'm thrown off. "I was just about to call you."

"Like you said goodbye?" He sounds hurt. "Well lucky for you, I beat you to it. This is more than just a one night stand, Kaitlin." Whoa. Snark does not suit him. My hackles rise as it dawns on me that I never told him where I work. On purpose. I didn't know who he was going to turn out to be, having met him online. And not in the mood to get murdered, or stalked. A chill runs down my spine.

"How did you get my work number and address?"

"I knew you said you worked today, and I thought you might like something pretty. How is your day going?"

"Greg." I pause to stress the importance of the question. I can't just file this away for later, like the money thing. He obviously has secrets that he is not ready to share. But so do I. "How did you get my work address and phone number?"

"I googled you." He seems embarrassed now. "I really had a good time last night. Are you mad at me?"

"Not mad. Just cautious." I relax momentarily. Yes, it is a little bit stalkerish but, I'm probably just freaking out with my past and all. "You could have just called me and asked me for my number at work or address saying you were going to send me flowers."

"If I had done that it wouldn't have been a surprise." He says cautiously. "And you might not have taken my call. I felt you last night, Kaitlin. When you got up and left. You didn't even try to say goodbye." He pauses, and the frantic tension in his voice almost melts me. "I don't want to scare you off. When can I see you again?" This all comes out to me in a rush of words. It's as if he's unsure of himself. Which doesn't really fit everything that I know about him. Greg seems to me a strong, vibrant man, who not only knows what he wants what is used to getting exactly what he wants, always, so the flowers at my workplace and number thing kind of makes sense. But the hesitancy in saying he wants to see me again doesn't really fit. I mean this guy is drop dead gorgeous, and I know for a fact, and in my heart of hearts, he could get any girl he wanted to. So why me?

"You want to see me again, huh?" I'm sure there's a smile in my voice.

"Don't tell me you didn't have fun last night. One of the things I love about you is your honesty, Kaitlin. And honestly, you know we fit together really well." He pauses, letting me feel the heat of his words. "Can I see you tonight?"

"No, I'm sorry. I'm afraid I've got so much work to do. Mrs. Jensen has a project that has a deadline that I've got to meet.

"Well, can I at least see you tonight for a coffee. I'm going to be heading out of town for a week tomorrow. And if I can't see you I really would like to talk to you before I go. Please?"

Filing away the stalkerish vibes. He really does seem like a sweet guy. I don't know why he wants to hang out with me. But I don't mind having a little fun.

"Yes. I'd like that. Coffee at 8? I'll text you my address."

"Great. Thank you." His excited puppy voice is back.

"Greg?"

"Yeah?"

"Do you already have my address?"

"Yes. Sorry." As quickly as his voice was high, now he seems almost fearful.

I smile to myself. I'm sure that wasn't on Google. What a fancy stalker I have.

"Just promise me you'll only use your power for good ok?"

"I promise. So… Coffee at 8?" He's hopeful now.

"Can't wait."

Chapter Five

I can't decide what to wear. I've been staring at my closet for about thirty minutes. I think I have narrowed it down to either the green sweater set or a long flowery dress. Ooh, or maybe the shirt dress. I rushed home to clean after a bumbling day with no focus at all. The hum of the vacuum soothed me, and I used the repetitive motion to think about the Greg situation. I mean, did I really believe it was going to be a one-time thing? Truthfully,I was just having fun messaging guys who I knew were way out of my league so I wouldn't have to worry about ever having to meet them. Welp, I guess I messed that up. I have a feeling that Greg is a little bit broken though too, and it is comforting. When we talked on the phone, he had shared with me that his parents were very distant and that it wasn't until he went away to school that he found anything close to what he would call a family. We talked about his friends and how he volunteers at a no-kill animal shelter. We talked a lot about him. I realize now that we didn't really talk as much about me. My excellent listening skills hid the fact, I hope. I think he kind of realizes that my past is a sensitive subject.

  See, six years ago I thought I was in love with Daniel, and he hurt me. He hurt me not just emotionally, but physically too. We were high school sweethearts, quickly married. It started out just verbally at first. He would tell me how I couldn't do anything right and belittle me. I thought it was because he was just having a rough time at work, because when it was worse at work, it seemed worse for me. I would even pray each night that he would have a good day. And whenever he had a long weekend he would shower me with attention and hold me and the world would be right again, it seemed. As a lawyer, he worked long hours, so when he said that he had to stay out late, I didn't think anything of it.

One day I noticed lipstick on his collar when I was doing the laundry. I gently pointed it out to him, and he said it was just a handsy eighty-year-old receptionist who I had met before. I believed him. And then things were peaceful again. For a while. It wasn't until he made partner that the physical abuse started. He was working even longer hours, and the only times I saw him was when he paraded me out to parties and events for the firm. Daniel kept me at his side all night, and I felt that we were the couple that we were in high school again. The jock and the bookworm, so it must be true love. Then when we got home, he reverted back into something else entirely. He would rip me apart for every little thing that he perceived that I did wrong that evening. Why didn't I smile more? Why didn't I talk to more people? 'I can't be with somebody so dull. You need to dress better. You need to work out more... Network. You need to network.' One night, I told him that I didn't want to go to a dinner party. I didn't like being treated like a monkey, paraded around for his friends. He grabbed me by my neck. He walked, pushing me back against the wall still holding me by my neck, essentially choking me. I froze. I didn't know how to respond. The next day I had marks on my neck. I had thought that he loved me. I loved him. At least I thought I did. The next day he was extremely apologetic and doted on me, saying that he was drunk the night before and he didn't know what he was doing.

I filed it away in the back of my mind praying that it never happen again. But that was just the first time.
That was the pattern. He would slap me, or choke me or, soon enough, punch me, and then he would be regretful and dote. Every time without fail. In the beginning at least. And then the apologies were further apart and the choking more and more frequent. Towards the end, if he moved his hand too quickly, I would cringe. As our relationship fell apart, I had less and less friends. The friends would comment about the way he was treating me, and I was so embarrassed that instead of leaving him, I left the friends, stopping talking to them. So when I did finally decide to leave, I left by myself in the middle of the night with nothing but a change of clothes and $200. I stayed a women's shelter for two nights. I moved across the country, as far away from him as I possibly could,I changed my last name, to start this new life that I live today. And I am so happy in this new life. Yes, I am lonely. But I am my own woman, and no one can tell me what to do.

A loud knocking at the door jolts me from my revelry. I look up from my clothing and realize that I am covered in tears, having begun crying while lost in the terrible memories of Daniel.

"Coming!" I yell across the room. I'm sure they can hear the shaking of my voice, I'm so emotional right now. I thought I was over and done with that time in my life. I rush to the door, looking through the peephole. Of course, it's Greg, who else would it be. Suddenly, I don't feel like seeing him tonight. The memories in my brain are raw and hurting, and I'm too sad at this moment to be any sort of company.

"Kaitlin? Are you okay?"
"I'm fine!" I shout through the door. "Really I'm feeling under the weather lately. Maybe we can talk when you come back to town?"
"Kaitlin." He pleads. I can tell that he is right against the door now. "Let me in." His voice holds so much emotion. It's comforting. Yes, I feel very comforted. As I open the door, he pushes it wide, quickly stalking inside and embracing me. Strong arms wrap around me and hold me tightly in a way that's smothering all the sadness. He holds me like this for what feels like an eternity, but still not long enough.
"What's wrong Katy baby?" He whispers into my temple with a dozen tiny kisses.
"Nothing. Nothing. I just don't feel well at all. I'm all right." My words are breathless and weak.
"You're not fine Katy baby. I can tell that easy enough. But if you don't want to talk about it, ok. I'll be here," he pauses to look into my eyes. "not talking about it with you, okay?" I look up into his beautiful ocean blue eyes and see a friend in my time of need. My vulnerability is making me seem weak, but at this moment I don't care. He's exactly what I need right now. I close the door and reach out to touch his face, the soft skin warm beneath my fingertips. Grabbing his head, I pull him down to me in a desperate kiss. I pour all into this. All the hurt, all the pain, all the yearning and sadness come out. And he kisses me back too. He is accepting what I'm giving him with patience and complete submission. He is allowing me to

take complete control the kiss. We move from the doorway to the couch. Pushing him on the sofa now strong and complete domination of the steps, I push him backward, grabbing his hair and kissing him deeply. My tongue thrusting, swirling in his mouth, completely and utterly taking what I need. I need this. I know that he can give it to me, this comfort. Taking a little bit of compassion. Taking away the sadness. Slowly, my kiss is transformed, as he begins to take control. Grabbing my hair he pulls my head back, arching my neck and thrusting deeply into my mouth, whirling around stroking the roof, pulling and nibbling on my lips. He trades positions with me, and now he is on top of me kissing me everywhere. He kisses my eyes, my neck, my ears, my chin. Wordlessly, he starts undoing the buttons of my dress.

Yes. This is what I need. I fumble for the buttons on his shirt. The clothing is flying now. No savoring or slow strip tease tonight. No 'Hi how are you?' He picks me up and carries me to my bedroom, thankfully visible from my living room because I know that words would fail me right now. He all but throws me on the bed, and I land artlessly with a thump. Reaching down with both hands he grabs my panties and in one quick movement, they are gone. Greg growls as he buries his face in my core with a loud wet kiss. His tongue delves deep, penetrating my folds and I buckle, bending in half with the intensity of this sensation. Instinctively, my legs try to close, and he pushes them wide growling as he does.

"Put your hands above your head." His voice is strong and unwavering. "Keep them there." Again by instinct alone, I obey, strangely, trusting him. I can feel the tension in his strong arms as he holds my legs apart. His motions gentle, and become more purposeful and thought out. He slowly nuzzles my clit. Slowly, so very slowly, he licks me delicately on that awesome bundle of nerves. It's too gentle. Not enough, yet still far too much. I feel as though every nerve in my body is turned on and electrified. I'm writhing now, moving restlessly, the tension building with no outlet. I can think of no other way to describe his actions but like that of someone thoroughly enjoying a meal. He takes his time, and I feel as though he is enjoying every second that he is down there, Which really makes me feel good. He releases my legs, which he had held at the knees. His hands gently stroke up my legs meeting in the center of me. As his talented lips continue the slow relentless exploring of me, his hands begin to slowly stroke my thighs, brushing gently from time to time across my nether lips. My eyes flutter closed, I am so enraptured by the sensation.

Whack! He has slapped my right thigh. I cringe at the sharp pain and jerk up, trying to shake him off of me. He grabs me quickly, holding my legs firmly in place. I lean up staring down at him in askance. His head is still lodged firmly between my legs, seemingly with no intention of budging. Looking into my eyes, in complete control, he kisses my clit, sucking hard. I almost snap in half, the pleasure is so intense. I'm dripping wet now, embarrassingly so. Again he nuzzles and licks at my center, gently kissing the lips with great care. I lean down again, trying to relax.

Whack! He slaps my left leg! This slap harder than the last. I try to shake him off.

"Hey!"

"Hands above your head Kaitlin." His gaze is intense but patient. "Trust me."
Again his blue eyes are a sea of calm as he looks right into my very soul, it seems as his lips latch and tug on my clit. That sharp pain morphs into a sweet burning pleasure, warming me from the outside in. In a strange opposition of sensation, he nuzzles and delicately kisses the button again. My orgasm hovers close now.
Whack! Whack! Whack! Whack! Whack! As swift, sharp blows rain down on the tender flesh of my thighs, he thrusts two fingers inside of me, curling them and stroking that perfect spot, opening the floodgate that is my orgasm. I'm flying and falling and shaking all at once, the pleasure is so intense.
Whack! Whack! Whack! Whack! Whack! As one hand administers sharp, hot strikes, talented fingers continue to thrust and curl and wring every last ounce of emotion and pleasure possible from me. I'm yelling and screaming now, calling his name in some kind of chant. As I think I'm about to descend, or ascend, or calm my jerking frame…
Whack! Whack! Whack! Whack! Whack!
He softly kisses my now red thighs, as talented fingers continue to thrust. His lips again latching on to my clit, suckle deeply and my orgasm starts all over again stretching on and on and on and on as if forever. He kisses up my center, stopping only for a moment to sheath himself quickly. Entering me fully in one sharp, long stroke, his thick cock kisses the tip of my womb. My face is dripping wet now, covered in tears of joy. My lips seek his, offering him all of my passion and pain. I smile into his mouth, in awe of his control. I know that I have had at least five orgasms now, and yet his

thrusts are completely controlled, long and smooth. Never ,ever have I had a man that cared so deeply about my pleasure that he put his side like this.

"Thank you." Feeling half sane again, after that full on assault to my senses, I clench my inner muscles, my effort to let him know I want him to feel this good too.
"Thank you." I squeeze again. Feeling his heartbeat in his chest as well as in his shaft, deep inside me, I continue to clench and grind against him.
"Thank you." I claw at his back, now focusing solely on him. I can somehow sense what he needs. My kisses become harsher, biting at his lips, before abandoning them altogether, to bite his ear, his neck, his chest. The further down I go, the harder the bites become. Feeling his urgency now, his motions becoming rushed, Feeling his frantic thrusts, and at the same time, this intense sensation of his pelvis thrashing against that wonderful bundle of nerves, tips me over the edge yet again. As my muscles begin to frenzy and spasm around him, I feel his release, the throbbing pulse of him going on and on as he holds on to me for dear life now. A shadow of pleasure pulses and I clench in aftershock, my inner muscles grabbing him, causing him to spasm as well. We laugh at the same time, completely lost in this intimacy. There is a long moment of peaceful quiet, as we bask in the afterglow.
"Hi." We both say at the same time.
"Jinx." Greg laughs and kisses me.

Chapter Six

It's been three whole days since I've last seen Greg. Turns out his trip is in Italy. I hate to say it, but I miss him dearly. So much for being just a one night stand.
After my vulnerable moment on Tuesday, where he rang me dry with orgasm after orgasm, he held me into the night and the next morning. He didn't make me talk, thank God. I don't know what would have happened if he had tried. He could sense that I had a wall around the subject and respected it.
"I just want you to know that I am here. If you need anything Katy, I'm here to bake cookies, or send flowers, or slay dragons if you need me to."

"I think this," I flipped in the bed to face him, trailing my hands down his warm chest, reveling in the slight sprinkling of hair. "was exactly what I needed."
"I get it." He returned seriously. I gasped as he grabbed me by my hair, bending my face to meet his gaze. "Talking can be tough. Just know that I'm good at other stuff too, like listening."
"Who said you were good?" I laughed into his mouth, playfully kissing him.
"As I recall, you were chanting 'thank you' for a while there…"

The phone rings, dragging me out of my daydream. Stupid phone. I rush across the room, half tripping on the sofa. Greg and I have been talking every night he's been away, so I hope it's him.

"Hey, Kaitlin. Channel seven, quick!" It's Jennifer, which isn't too unusual. Even though I am a homebody, sometimes she will call so randomly with gossip or a question from her drama queen life. Sometimes I feel like her big sister, but in a good way.

"What for?"

"You have to turn on the t.v. right now. Mrs. Jensen says she wants you to get a look at a new client and get some ideas. She has commissioned an original design. You are never gonna believe who you'll be making it for! OMG! Never!"

"I kinda am expecting a call." I look at the clock. It's almost nine. Greg will be calling any minute now.

"OMG! SHUT THE FUCK UP AND TURN TO CHANNEL SEVEN! You need to do this now, because she may be coming in as soon as tomorrow!"

I turn on the t.v. to channel seven. It's a red carpet movie event of some sort. This is big. Mrs. Jensen designs dresses for celebrities all the time, but this is the first time I've been asked to get ideas for one. I know she had been using a lot of my designs lately. This really is exciting. Maybe I'll get to be the lead designer on this.

"So who am I looking for?"

"Wait for it. She should be on any second. She is only the hottest thing right now. Here she comes! Tiffany Darling!" Jennifer makes a loud squeal into the phone.

"You know I don't watch much t.v. What is she wearing? What does she look like?"

"The tiny blonde who is about a third the way down now. She is wearing the pearl Versace lace with a plunging back. You could do better, though. And she has the hottest piece of billionaire man candy on the planet on her arm. Derek G. Weathering! OMG! Couldn't you just eat him with a spoon?"

I can finally see the lady in question. However, I just can't take my eyes off of her doting date. Six foot four, Blonde hair, blue eyes. Killer smile that could stop a train.

Suddenly I feel very, very faint.

"Derek Gregory Weathering?"

Greg...

End of part one…

And now a Sneak Peak of Part 2…
Billionaire Boyfriend
December 2016

Billionaire Boyfriend
A Billionaire Bad Boys Steamy Romance Book 2
By Elyse Young

So… it appears that my new, sort of boyfriend is a Billionaire… a famous one. The kind of famous that courts tabloids and rumor – something I would have known about if I bothered to watch TV, or if he had bothered to tell me…

Nothing about this makes sense and my head is spinning. Who would've thought that a dating app could lead me here? That doesn't happen in real life! Greg is darn near perfect; sweet, funny and sexy as sin. And while not telling me about his rich man status isn't exactly a deal breaker, his ex (current??) girlfriend just might be. Add in my own troubled ex, Daniel, and a past I would rather forget and suddenly I am not so sure this fairy tale is going to be my happily ever after, after all.

Fans of J.S. Scott, Penny Wylder and E.L. James are sure to love the fun, sexy style of Elyse Young! Billionaire Boyfriend picks up where Billionaire Blind Date leaves off, continuing this naughty adventure that will inspire the romantic, and vixen, in all of us.

Billionaire Boyfriend
by Elyse Young

Chapter One

Warm fingers caress my face. He is kissing me. Blue oceans of desire stare intently at me. He is asking me a question I do not know the answer to. I close my eyes and bask in the feeling, as strong hands glide from my face down to caress my neck and shoulders, pausing only briefly at my breasts before delving further down. My skin sparks deliciously as kisses rain down where his hands had been. I am drenched in sensation, not so much of arousal, as of comfort and care. It's as if he's showing me how much he cares with all of his actions. His head dips lower now, nuzzling at my very core. Suddenly a hand slaps down on my thigh, shocking and stinging me. This is different than the other night, though. Before was perfect. It was just what I needed, releasing of all the sorrow and pain I had been holding onto for so long. With his instinctive sexual prowess, I was finally able to let go... This, this touch... is scary. This slap is violent. It's as if he is punishing me, but I do not know what for. The pain is searing and intense, and I am fearful of him for the first time. What have I done? I wince again thinking to myself. It's not the first time I've asked this question, but it is the first time I've asked this question with Greg. The blinding pain finally ceases, and he rises up to look into my eyes again, this time his blue eyes are dark as midnight ocean, no longer filled with love but with disgust. He turns from me to the other woman beside us in the bed. She is a vision of beauty, blonde and feminine and tiny and the very essence of a whole woman. As she looks over at me, baring her teeth in a possessive smile, I'm jolted awake. Ice cold sweat coats my body.

It's been several years since I've had the nightmares. Not since Daniel. After last night's revelations, I can understand why I have them, though. I look down my cell phone beside my bed. 3:30 a.m. I also see that I've missed 10 calls. 9 from Greg, or should I say Derek Gregory Weathering, Billionaire Banking Mogul, and one from Jennifer. I don't know what to do with myself. I was just hoping to live in a boyfriend bubble for just a little bit longer. I knew something was off. My blind date, 'Greg' assured me that he was single. And I knew he had money, not that I care. Yes, going from being a virtual spinster to going out with a billionaire with a "B" is a bit more intense than I was planning for when I tried out the dating app, but… It was going so well. He, like myself, was a homebody. With what little I knew of him, which, I think, is a lot more than I know about most of the guys that I have dated in my life. I believed that he didn't like the limelight. But what I can't stand for was him lying about not being with anyone else. I cannot stand for cheating. When Jennifer told me to quickly turn on the TV, I just thought I'd be checking out a new client to get a sense of her style.

When I saw Greg, with his arms wrapped around the movie star Tiffany Darling, my body went cold. My heart froze. I've been cheated on before with my ex, Daniel and I will not do it again. He could have told me... If he had just been honest with me... Well, I guess I would have ended it. But, at least it would have been better than this hard tight feeling I have in my chest right now. I guess it's better to have found out now rather than later. I had told myself that it was supposed to just be a fling and now, I guess the fling has been flung. I turn my phone upside down where I cannot see it and wearily lay my head back down, praying for sleep

Chapter Two

I can't help but smile as my adorable self-adopted little sister Jen, smiles brightly up at me clutching onto a cup of coffee in a tiny coffee shop a few blocks from work, happy for a Monday for the first time ever. Not quite glad that the weekend is over, as she is happily waiting for the details of my 'torrid' affair.
"Not so much a torrid affair, Jen. More like a blind date that turned out to be, I don't know, him, I guess."
"OMG billionaire blind date! Kaitlin, tell me all about 'Greg'! You can't say you didn't realize you were dating THE billionaire Derek Gregory Weathering?"
"You know I don't watch much TV. And he introduced himself to me as just Greg." I know I'm getting defensive now, I can't help it. "And come to think of it, when he sent me his pictures, they were all of someone who kind of looked like him. You know tall, blonde and handsome, but not quite him, specifically. I was just thinking maybe he had reservations about putting himself online. I mean, I could totally understand that. I really wasn't comfortable putting myself out there like that either."
"I am so jelly that you found him and not me! It sucks that he turned out… well... But I'm glad that you are getting back out there. So what that he proved to be a jerk… there are plenty of fish in the sea."
I clutch my sugar-free mocha for dear life, taking comfort in feeling the warmth seep into my skin slowing.
We sit in silence for a moment. When she reaches across the table to hold my hand,I can feel tears prick at the back of my

eyes, begging to be freed. I will not cry, though. He does not deserve my tears.

"So… what are you going to do about today? You know… his girlfriend? I mean, are you sure she is even his girlfriend? They might just be friends? You know how Hollywood gossip can be."

"I'm pretty sure. I did a Google search afterward and found a lot of pictures of them together, in some they were even kissing. And an article asking if America's most eligible bachelor is finally off the market."

"What I don't understand is why was he on a dating website in the first place. Oh! I have an idea!" Jennifer begins bouncing quickly in her seat."Why don't you tell her what he has been up to? You know, let him know that playing with people's emotions isn't cool. Ooh! I bet we could sell the story to TMZ!"

"No!" I shout a little too violently. I thought about it that night for quite a while. After tossing and turning and that horrible dream, I came to a decision. No, I am not going to rat him out. I am, however, going to let him know how I feel about being lied to. And I am not going to jeopardize my opportunity to take the lead on a custom couture dress destined for the runway. After doing a little research on Tiffany Darling, I'm sure she's an awesome girl. She just didn't know she was dating a slimebag.

"No, I would hate to do anything without knowing the whole story. Plus I don't want to put Ms. Darling in the spotlight and jeopardize my opportunity to take the lead on that Couture dress." Jennifer reaches over yet again and squeezes my hand.

"Don't worry girl! I've got your back. You ready for work?" And with that, we head out the door, ready to begin again.

Josh, is perched on my workstation when I arrive at work, holding two cups of coffee. I can't help but grin.

"Is one of those for me?"

"Sugar-free vanilla and cream with Splenda, just how you like it." He smirks at me flashing pearly white teeth.

"How do you know how I like it?" What's this all about?

"I have my ways. His fingers gently brush mine as he hands me the cup. My breath catches.

"What's this for?" My work crush, Josh has never been this friendly before, let alone flirty. Has my time with Greg changed me?

"Just for that beautiful smile that I love seeing on your face. How about happy hour tonight after work, you know, to celebrate you taking the lead on this big assignment?" Hmm, I have never done happy hour with the crew before...

"You know what?" I puff my chest out and feel a bit proud of myself. "I'd love to."

"Well, Ok!" he seemed shocked and yet very proud of himself . He kisses me tenderly on my cheek before heading back up to the front desk. Whoa! "Mrs. Darling will be in at 10 a.m!" He shouts as he walks out.

Time flies by in a whirlwind of sketches as I am putting together ideas for THE Miss Tiffany Darling. I am so excited! I know, my emotions are a bit mixed with the whole Greg, or should I say Derek situation, but I really AM excited to be taking the lead for the 1st time. A knock at the door grabs my attention and I lift my head up from my sketches. "Yoo Hoo darling! Oh, no worries! It's just me Darling." Mrs. Jensen pops her head in. She is a woman of great refinement, English, in her late fifties, but looking like a young 40. Well preserved and elegant. Slender and tall with blonde hair and the tiniest bit of silver. She is the picture of posh.

"I just wanted to make sure everything is on track for Miss Darling."

"Everything is well, Mrs. Jensen. And I'm very happy and excited that you've given me this opportunity."

"Pish, posh! You know that you are more than ready for this. In fact, I wanted to give you this." She hands me a check. Wow. Six thousand dollars! "The last run of designs you did for me has done exceedingly well, & I wanted to make sure you knew how valued you are to me. You know," She leans close to me her voice becomes wistful. "I won't be around doing this forever. And I would like to think of you as my protege. I always appreciate your work dearest, Kaitlin. Would you consider making this more of your passion and taking over when I decide I'm ready to retire?"

I'm quite sure my fair skin is beet red, and my mouth is hanging open. I cannot believe this.

"Of course Mrs Jensen, I will be more than happy to! Please! Let me know whatever it is you need for me to do to prepare myself."

"Now, don't get too excited. It will be a bit before I decide to take the final steps, but in the coming months I will be asking a bit more of you." She delicately perches on the edge of my desk. Reaching down she strokes a fleck of something off my cheek staring lovingly . "I do want to keep the name of

Mrs. Jensen's alive a bit longer. Perhaps," She hesitates briefly, "you should take a minute to freshen your face, Darling, I believe miss Tiffany Darling is due in about a half of an hour. Perhaps a bit of gloss?" she raises her eyebrows high, and I realize the suggestion is more of a command. I nod slowly in acquiescence. "Splendid, Dear. You have a pleasant day!"

I look in the mirror at my reflection. I thought I looked acceptable when I left the house this morning. But I guess that almost crying for the last few days does have me looking a bit drab. My light complexion is beet red and flushed from all that has happened. My hair, golden red curls hang limply in a loose ponytail with the back of my neck. I personally do not care, but I guess I now should represent Mrs. Jensen by looking my best. I rummage through my purse searching for a lipstick, hoping that I have one there. I settle on a Carmex. As that is all that I can find. I also find an eyebrow pencil which I use to tame my brows. Then thinking on it decide to use it to spruce my eyes a bit as a liner. The phone rings and I answer automatically. "Mrs. Jensen's? This is Kaitlin speaking. How can I help you?"

"Kaitlin?" The warm, strong voice lighting my insides belongs to Greg. My breath is frozen as I slam the receiver down. I'm not ready for this conversation. The phone rings again. I answer the phone lifting it from the receiver but saying nothing.

"Katy baby?" His voice is shaky, scared even. "What's wrong? Have I done something wrong?" I feel freezing suddenly.

"I didn't answer my cell phone, Greg, because I didn't want to talk to you." I'm very surprised how calmly my words come out. "Please don't call me at work."

"Wait! Don't hang up. Please! Please! What. Is. Wrong. Tell me!" The strength and force of his words anger me and still me at the same time.

"Well Derek," I state his real name in a clipped tone. "I saw you on TV."

There's silence, and for a moment I hold my breath, waiting to see what he will say.

"Oh." A long moment passes. "I wanted to tell you. Just…" There is a long moment of silence while he finds his words. "You said money didn't matter."

"You think this is about money?" I almost laugh in anger. "You know I don't care about money. This is about Tiffany Darling and the fact that you told me that you were single."

"I am single! Tiffany and I dated a long time ago, and we're still friends. I was down in Italy closing a major deal, and she happened to call me saying that her companion canceled at the last minute and asked me if I would help her out by attending some event." His words are rushed, excited, and nervous. I feel like I should believe him. There really is no reason for him to lie to me. I mean, who would care about keeping me when you have Tiffany Darling? "Really Kaitlin, for the life of me I don't even know what event I attended. The second it was over, I couldn't wait to get back to my hotel and call you. You are who I choose to spend my time with. You know this." the gentle passion behind his words softens me. Another pause. "Don't you know this?"

" I don't know what I know. I don't even know what to call you. Should I call you Derek now? Or does anyone else in this world call you Greg?"

"You call me Greg. You are the one... who knows the real me."

"But that's just it. I don't know you. There are little pieces missing from your story. I don't know enough to even ask what they are."

"You know me. You know more than anyone else in this world. And I think... I think I know you too." His voice is small, but it commands me, begs me, touches me. "I know that you're hiding, Kaitlin. I know that you were hurt before. And I know that you're looking for any reason to not see me again." I am breathless now, have I held my breath? I am overwhelmed with the heavy feeling in my chest from his words... Do I dare believe that this strange, beautiful man wants me?

"Let's start over. Please?" Though he means it to sound light, that please is as heavy as stone. There's an echo of silence, his breath held an eternity awaiting my response. He pushes on. "Hi, my name is Greg. A lot of people call me Derek Gregory Weathering, though. But I'd like for you to call me Greg. Is that okay?" I laugh, for the first time since he held me the other day. It feels likes that were years ago.

"Hi, Greg. I'm Kaitlin. Pleased to meet you." There's a silence and the energy changes in the call. It becomes heated and intense. I can feel him calming, and his power spikes a longing in my core.

"Tell me I can see you tonight." A plea and command all at once.

"I can't. I promised I would go to happy hour after work with my coworkers. We're celebrating. Actually," I pause trying to decide if I should say anything. "Tiffany Darling is a new client of ours. I have a meeting with her in just a few minutes."

"Really? What a coincidence." He sounds angry. "Can I see you after?" He's puppy dog anxious now.

"Of course. I'll meet you at my place… Say 9 o'clock tonight?"
"I don't think I can wait that long… hey," he pauses briefly, and I hold my breath. "Thank you."
"For what?" This gentleness is a side to him I don't think many folks see.
"For trusting me. I know that takes a lot."
And just like that, we are us again. It's as if he can see the inside of me all the way down to what I am not saying.

Chapter Three

"She's here, she's here, she's here!"

Jennifer bounds in the door bouncing up and down excitedly. Funny, something I was so excited about before is now making me very nervous. The story was a bit different when I thought that my relationship with Greg was over and I would be working with his girlfriend. I don't know why I didn't think that was awkward, but this, this I think is much more awkward. The fact that I will be working with Greg's ex-girlfriend. At least she doesn't know about me. That would be really... awkward. I check my reflection, fixing my eyes once more. When I reach the private salon, Mrs. Jensen is entertaining a tiny woman. Wow. Tiffany Darling looks totally different in person. If possible, she is even more feminine. She stands at 5'5" in 4" heels, so she is really like 5'1". Her platinum blonde hair looks natural, with the tiniest bit of strawberry. Her nose is petite and slightly upturned, and her lips are full and lush with the cutest cupid's bow. Next to her, I feel like a giant swamp troll.

When she sees me, her face transforms to that of a child at Christmas. Excited to see me?

"Kaitlin! I so happy that you are available to see me on such short notice!" She practically floats across the room and clasps my hands. "Why, just the other day I was in Italy, and a good friend of mine was telling me about your wonderful designs… as I'm sure they have told you, I have been offered the opportunity to present last minute at an award show, and my stylist has ended up… unavailable. Thank you a thousand times!"

"It really is my pleasure to assist. Tell me, who referred you?"
"A good friend and old beau, Derek Weathering." She is looking at me closely now, searching, I guess for my response. Which is easy. My response is that of relief. I still am not quite sure how much of what Greg told me was the truth. I'm euphoric now to hear that they are completely done. She said good friend, right?
"Well, I'll have to thank Mr. Weathering when next I see him." She visibly calms at my lack of familiarity when addressing him. Good.
"Shall we begin?"
"Oh absolutely! I was thinking of something in the purple family?"

The meeting was a fun one. Turns out she loved my sense of style and embraced almost all of my suggestions. We did the fitting, and she commissioned a second dress from me as well.
Tiffany is a really great girl. After you get over the fact that she is a mega star, she has a very girl next door feel to her. She's sweet, polite and friendly. As our meeting came to a close, I felt almost like I had made a new friend. I didn't have the bravery to ask her about Greg. She didn't volunteer any information either.
The rest of the day flew by. I was working on sketches and looking at fabric for her dress for the award show. Then I quickly set to the task of handling my other duties. The figurative whistle blows, and it's 5 o'clock. I'm exhausted yet really energized. I can't wait for happy hour to tell Jen all about my meeting with miss Tiffany Darling.

'The Watering Hole,' the bar that sits across the street from Mrs. Jensen's is a great hangout spot for the after work business crowd. There are big screen TVs everywhere for sports. The bar is large and dark and very woodsy. A very manly bar. Which explains why they're all these suits in here. Misses Jensen's is tucked away in the financial district downtown, and we are surrounded, us clothiers, by bankers and architects and the like. Wow. If I wasn't with Greg now, I really could come down here and have a cocktail and do some people watching one day. Greg. Maybe I should keep this happy hour short to get home. I haven't cleaned my house in a minute. I keep getting interrupted by sketch ideas. We sit at a large booth in the back, myself, Jennifer, Josh, Teddy from the front office, Jim who is one of our fabric suppliers, and Tim, who handles our deliveries. It has been a fun hour so far. I've had a girlie martini that Jennifer turns me on too called the Ladies Manzana. It's lovely and sweet with gin and cognac. I don't tend to drink much, and when I do I like wine, but this really is hitting the spot. I feel warm and light and very happy as to how the day is gone so far. I look up when a drink is gently placed in front of me, red wine. Josh smiles down at me.
"I thought this was more your speed."
"Thank you."
"It's a Malbec, right?" How does he know that? "Yes I love Malbec, thank you."
"Congrats again little girl." He kisses me on the cheek. Really?! Twice in one day. I wonder what's up. I'm sure I'm blushing. I turn, looking to Jennifer for her thoughts. She just shrugs her shoulders at me smiling.

I am startled, and aroused, sensing him before I see him . A warm hand clamps down on my shoulder, a little too firmly. "Am I late, Honey?" Greg's voice sounds rough and gravely against my ear. I see his hand is also on Josh's shoulder. Greg is staring at Josh intently, and not in a nice way.
"I thought you were meeting me later tonight, right?"
"I thought I'd surprise you. Surprised?" It seems to be a real question. And his eyes are practically sparks. "Introduce me to your friends, sweetie." Honey, Sweetie? Did we skip some steps here? What is up with all these endearments? This is the first time we have ever been out in public besides that first time at the coffee shop. Weird.
"Ok? Well, that's Josh. He works at the front desk. This," I point my head to the side "is Jennifer, one of my best friends. She's also a designer." I gesture around the table with my hand, "We have Jim, Teddy, and Tim. Everyone, this is... "
"Her boyfriend, Derek Weathering. Hi, great to meet you everyone." he wraps an arm possessively around me squeezing slightly. Boyfriend? Derek? What the hell!? Really. Caveman much? I hold my tongue but stare daggers at him. He's kissing me territorially on the forehead, and I can't see it, but I can feel death rays focused at Josh. If I weren't me and he wasn't him, I might even think he was jealous.
"I'd like to get the tab tonight. After all, we are celebrating my girl's achievement!" He's holding me tightly now, and his warmth and wonderfully woodsy scent are almost overbearing. I feel smothered. But the sensation is... Nice. Almost like he's a doting boyfriend, even though I know better. This is obviously some sort of testosterone fueled pissing contest with Josh, I'm sure. But, with his arms wrapped around me and him hovering so very tall above,

Josh, who, standing across from us seems slight by comparison, really just a boy. If I thought that Greg was sexy in jeans and a t-shirt, well, it's nothing compared to the powerhouse threat that is Greg in a suit. Today he is wearing a fitted Armani, that hugs him like a lover, highlighting his broad shoulders and his lean waist. His 6'4" frame towering above everyone and his soft blonde hair sculpted to a sleek business style. So sharp, it just reminds me of its usual surfer boy freedom and taunts me to run my fingers through it, mussing him and staking my claim to all of the ladies nearby who are just as mesmerized as I am. Sitting as I am, which is having been hauled into his lap, my back against his broad, hot chest, his rigid arousal poking the now overly sensitized skin where my lower back meets my ass, I wonder idly if he can tell how wet I am. I feel like I'm in a pool of my own lust. It's his fault. As he wraps his arms around me, he is discreetly brushing the soft underside of my breasts, something I didn't know was that sensitive until just now.
"Would you all excuse me for a moment? I think I need the little girls."
"Ooh! I'll come too!" Jennifer rises to join me and the gentleman part like the sea, aware that the girlie gossip fest is about to begin. Greg releases me, begrudgingly, grabbing me by the shoulders to face him. He kisses me. *Whoa!* This is not just some playful peck, but a full on assault to my senses. He captures my head, grabbing my hair for control, tilting me for better access. He plunders my mouth, delving inside, to lick and suckle and explore. I am so dazed by the attack, so caught up in the heat and electricity, that I respond fully, forgetting for the briefest moment that we are surrounded by my co-workers. It's Greg who, finally ends the kiss, and I am

so embarrassed. I'm sure I look like a panting, blotchy red mess. I look up, amazed, into his eyes and see dark blue triumph. He's smiling into my mouth now. One last peck and he releases me. I wobble wordlessly to the restroom, my legs shaky, and my core a slippery mess.

"Wow, wow, wow. Just wow, Kaitlin. I thought he was gonna sock Josh in the jaw! What the hell! Why did you just let him kiss you? I thought you were going to tell him off?" Jennifer is bursting with curiosity.
"It's not quite as bad as you think. It's still pretty bad, but… Ok . Listen. It turns out he and Tiffany Darling are exes for quite some time. I freaked out over nothing." I'm shaking now. I may even be hyperventilating. "She even told me that it was Greg who mentioned my work to her. So I know he isn't lying… but that pissing contest?! He was acting like he owned me! And this is the first time we have been out in public. What is he thinking?"
"He thinks that you are his girl!" Jennifer is literally jumping up and down with excitement. "He is marking you so that every other man in the room knows. And it was HOT. Tell me he was awesome in bed. Please tell me! Lie if you have to!"
I laugh. If she only knew the half of it. Looking into her big green puppy dog eyes, all I can do is nod furiously. "So he is your boyfriend now? I mean, that is a pretty ballsy label for someone you were never setting eyes on again as of earlier today, right?"
"That's what I'm saying!" I shout. "He can't just show up and pee all over me!"

"But it was HOT, though, just saying…" her voice is wistful, and she shrugs her shoulders. Now we are both smiling and burst into a fit of giggles.

When we return to our seats, it seems as though Greg has won over the guys. I catch only the tail end of it, but it sounds like they are all going to an LA Kings game soon.
"Yeah, me and my brother try to get tickets every time they are in town. Thanks, man!" That pleasant voice is none other than Josh, who just minutes ago was this close to getting decked. What? Now they are best buds? Ok. I guess Greg's charm is not only good on women.
"What are we talking about?" I squish in and tuck myself into Greg's side, enjoying the sudden PDA closeness that I have been granted access to.

As I settle comfortably again in Greg's lap, a server arrives with two bottles of Dom Perignon. *Woo-hoo. Fancy.*
"A toast, in honor of Kaitlin and her soon to be one of a kind couture design!" He leans close to whisper, "I plan on celebrating my girl thoroughly tonight. I missed you." His words are wet and warm on my ear. My dumb womb clenches conspiratorially. His hand caresses my arm, and I shiver...

The air is icy as we walk to his town car, where his driver waits for us. It feels like Christmas to me at this moment, all bright and protected. I have had enough time to think, as I was sitting and listening to the boys talk sports, and feeling the amazing patterns being drawn on my skin, when Greg could not keep his hands off of me. I am definitely not as angry as I was before at his possessiveness. I mean I know I'm not 21 anymore. I guess the label of "boyfriend" this soon will not kill me. And it's not like anyone is beating down my door for a date. So if he wants to try dating me, I'm willing to give it a go. I was worried that him being a billionaire would be really scary because of his profile. But hanging out with him at happy hour seemed calm. It's not like we were attacked by paparazzi at the sports bar. I guess that's the nice thing about LA. mewing around everywhere. So what if his starts with a B?

We sit in companionable silence as we are driven towards the Hollywood hills… Wait what?

"Where do you think that we are going, Greg?" I try to sound calm.

"Home." He gently kisses me. Sweet, really.

"I told you." I try to begin lightly, "I would meet you at my place tonight at nine." I pull away from him to look in his eyes. "How does that translate into 'Please crash my work event and drag me to your Mansion Hideaway?" The look he gives me burns my skin, it is so searing. He gets very, very close and the air around us heats to the point that I can barely breathe. Grabbing me by my hair he tilts my head back, angling me for a deep kiss. I wait, holding my breath for the impact, but it never comes. He just gets so close that our lips are almost, almost touching as he says,

"I haven't seen you, felt you, held you, in days." He pauses briefly allowing the impact of his words to resonate. "You tried to leave me without so such as a goodbye. And when I do see you, there is another man all. over. you." His words start calm but then build in intensity. At the end, his volume drops to nothing but a gravelly whisper against my skin. " He kissed you."

"On the cheek!" My response is an excited whisper. This much almost kissing, while he says these kinds of things to me, has my body in a frenzy. My nipples peak, brushing against him and I bite my lip, stifling a groan.

"He. Kissed. You. I am taking you to my home Kaitlin." He tightens his grip on my hair, forcing my head to tilt back further still. "I'm going to do what I've been dying to do all night. Which is to fuck you thoroughly. And when I make you come, I want you screaming my name so loud that the wolves howl." He moves from my lips to my ear, gently biting. "I am taking what is mine, and I am going to mark you in so many ways that they will know that you're are mine from outer space."

He kisses me now, and the impact of his words, and his heat and his virility are too much for me to stand. I open for him, and he plunges and plunders my mouth thoroughly, sucking on my tongue and making me writhe beneath him. Teeth tug at my lips, and he laves at me, feasting on me, a starving man.

"So, I'm Your's, huh?" Sated, I whisper. He nods his head gently and kisses me softly again. "You don't think that's a little fast?"

"You feel this Kaitlin. Do not try to deny me." He reaches between my legs, cupping my sex and squeezing. "This... is mine." Tilting my head back, he devours my mouth again. I am so close to coming. I don't know how I feel about this side to Greg. Domineering, but really hot.

"Who's is this Kaitlin?" He squeezes again, grinding his palm into that sweet, hot, wonderful spot, spiking my pleasure. Lightning quick, he hitches up my skirt plunging his fingers inside me. They curl stroking that precious spot quickly and with precision. Just as quickly, they are gone. I teeter on the edge of a powerful climax. My mouth agape, my body curling, almost in pain at its intensity. His lips touch my ear as he whispered softly, "Answer me. Whose is this, Kaitlin?" My only response is a violent moan as he continues to rub slow circles on my clit.

"Is this Josh's? Does this belong to Josh?" He spits the words at me. I'm panting now. "No. This doesn't belong to Josh, does it?" he bites my ear, gently licking and nibbling, sucking on the flesh of my ear and neck.

"And is this yours? Does this belong to you, Kaitlin?" I shake my head yes. "No. This," His hand swats my center, making me jump. "This is mine now. Say it. Say it!" His strong fingers spear me again, and His palm is grinding faster and faster and faster, and I tip violently, gloriously over the edge into a powerful, intense, shuttering pool of pleasure. But he doesn't stop. He keeps on going, grinding at the perfect speed. His other hand reaches for my breast, squeezing gently, pulling at my nipples through my clothes.

"Say it Kaitlin. Tell me this is mine. Tell me, baby." Now more of a pleading whimper, than a command. "Whose is this Kaitlin?"

"It's yours! It's yours!" The words become a chant. My orgasm continues to crest, going on and on for what seems like forever. "Say my name, baby. Please say my name! Say Greg!"

"It's yours, Greg! It's your's Greg. Greg! Greg!" I continue to chant softer and softer as I begin to come down from my beautiful high, breathless now… " Greg. Greg. Greg…"

"God, you are so beautiful. I can't tell you how much I needed that, Katy baby." He holds me close now, inhaling my scent. "So, what do you want for dinner?" He Grins. "I'm thinking pizza?"

Chapter Four

After his abrupt topic change, I am completely frozen. He's holding me tightly, and we ride in silence. He is stroking my hair like a puppy and seems pretty proud of himself. I, however.am freaking out, totally stunned by the last ten minutes. I feel like I have been pleasured to silence. We arrive at his place, a beautiful home in the hills of Hollywood. Though I've seen it before, it still stuns me with its tranquillity. Large open spaces, koi ponds in front and gorgeous wood furnishings throughout. As we enter, his huge Rottweiler, Honey, bounds down to greet us.
"Hi, Honey, I'm home." I crouch down to pet her.
He crouches and strokes her head.
"Did you miss Kaitlin too, Honey, huh? Yea, but not as much as I did." I am still stunned speechless. I thought I was ok with his possessiveness, but after what happened in the town car, I am out of my depth.
He guides me to the den, grabbing an afghan on the way. Depositing my on a plush leather couch, I think he is grinning just the slightest, and he is biting on his lower lip to the point of distraction.
"Ok. I'm ready." He takes my hands and holds them, drawing patterns with his thumbs.
"What?"
"I know. I was being bad. Let me have it."
"What?" I say again confused.
"I know I went off in there, but when I saw that guy kissing you? What the fuck, Kaitlin?" His gaze is piercing, his beautiful blue eyes assessing me, assessing my reaction. "I

thought I handled myself pretty well." He pulls his hair, messing it. "And I want to talk about the fact but you saw something on TV and were just never going to speak to me again. Is that right? Do you not think what we're sharing right now is important, special? Well?" Somehow he's turned this on me saying it's all my fault?

"You lied to me Greg, or Derek, or whatever. I don't care. Do you get that? I don't care that you have got lots of money. You care that I'm a seamstress? You know this. What I care about is the fact that you had a girlfriend. And went out with her and said nothing to me. That is what I care about." He puts a finger to my lips, silencing me.

"Exactly. Without even hearing my side of the story, you just as assume that I'm in Italy cheating on you."

"How can you be cheating on me, when we aren't a couple?

"Katy, baby, we have been a couple since the moment I laid eyes on you." His voice drops, low and rough. He pulls me now onto his lap, cupping my head, his fingers in my hair, holding, gripping me. "In fact, we were a couple even before then, since the first time I heard your voice you have been mine. I want you. You want me. Why are you trying to make this complicated? Let's just do it. Ok?" My spine registers a chill, but my skin is burning at his proclamation.

"Greg, I don't know if I'm ready for anything serious right now. I have been hurt in the past…" my sentence dies in my throat, my body physically refusing to release my fears. I lay my head in the cradle of his neck, hiding. I'm not ready to end this, but I know Greg is the kind of man who won't settle for half measures. To my surprise, he kisses my hair and says, "I know." He lifts my chin so that we are staring into each other's eyes. "I'm broken too. I'm just happy you can't see it

yet. I've been hurt too. In fact," he takes a deep breath, squaring his shoulders. I want to talk to you about Tiffany."
"What about Tiffany?"
"She and I have a troubled past." He says as if that's only half the story. "She broke my heart, but it's not like you think. When we were dating, we started out as just going to functions together as friends,. And then it became more serious when our families got involved." He pauses thoughtfully. "Our Parents really wanted to see us together. From the outside, we were the perfect power couple. Because I was being pressured so much by my mother, I just acquiesced. Resigned that it was a match for money and not love." His laugh is like a soft bark… "She cheated on me multiple times." His eyes move back and forth searching struggling, looking for the right words. "She would flaunt it in my face when I found out. I don't know how to put this delicately. She has... issues. I don't think you should trust her. I don't know why she is working with you, other than that you're a great designer. But I can't help think she's up to something." The sting is only brief, lessened by the impact of his confession.
"That's funny. She had nothing to say about you, except that you used to date. In fact, that's the reason why we're talking right now. If she hadn't said that to me... I don't know that we would be talking at all right now." I try to take a moment to breathe and think… where do we go from here? "You deal in half truths, Greg. I don't feel like I can trust you."
"Well," he pauses, ocean blue eyes capturing my green, "I don't know if I can trust at all." he grabs my hair suddenly, roughly, tipping my head back and devouring my mouth. There's absolutely no question that this is a claiming. Not

gentle, not caring. This, is his beast, claiming mine. My womb clinches. As much as I know, we need to finish this conversation I also know that his hot breath in my face is pleading silently to fill the void that I feel just as strongly as he does. The fight will be there an hour, right? Now, the raw feeling that burns every inch of my flesh is being soothed by the ferocity of this kiss. His lips scrape and pull at mine. His strong hands control the angle of my head, tipping me backward, granting deeper access so that his tongue can explore the warm depths of me. With each stroke, I feel the intensity building. I let go. Pushing him back, I crawl on him grabbing his hair with too much force, tipping his head back revealing his muscular neck. Reveling in my power, the power of things between us. I am like an animal. I bite and suckle on the flesh of his neck, feasting on his heady scent, warm and spicy and mint and musk. He growls, picking me up without separating. He begins walking towards his bedroom, and I burst into a fit of giggles. I have never had anyone carry me before. I'm 5 foot 9. I have never been a delicate flower. I wrap my legs around his waist, as up, up, up the stairs we go, me and my cave man. No, he doesn't break his stride or lose his breath. Reaching the top, our rabid makeout session has turned into the soft nuzzling on each other's necks and ears. Entering his room, I am thrown unceremoniously on the bed. I can't help it. I burst into another fit of giggles again after catching my breath from the loud thunking noise my body makes on his mattress.

Sitting up I begin to peel off my too many layers of clothes, suddenly hot everywhere. Greg pounces on me, assisting in strokes. I think it's an attempt to soothe me. Suddenly his nails sink into my flesh , scratching me.

"Agh!" I cry out, more from shock than from pain.

"Yes, Kaitlin. I want you to let everything out."

His tongue laves wetly at my now searing flesh, calming the sting. His lips find my right breast, and he gently nips and licks all around stroking every inch of my flesh, except where I need it most, my aching nipples. I moan in frustration as he does the same with my left. My nipples peak and harden to throbbing pebbles completely ignored. The music grows louder, so loud that I can no longer hear Greg, or even the sound of my own breathing. He steps away, and I relax, the calming drone of Spanish guitar allowing my mind to let go of thought. I am nothing but an ocean of feeling, every nerve in my body waiting for his next move. I wait so long, in fact, I heart beat slows. Though I can still feel it's rhythm throughout my body, it's calmer now. I sense Greg's heat approach me again, and I smile. I'm ready, I think. Firm pressure grips my nipples, tightening more and more. It's not his fingers, though… Clamps? I bite my lip, holding in a shriek. He twists them now, releasing the slightest bit of pressure. That somehow causes them to throb more painfully. I whimper. Kissing down my torso, he reaches the center of me. I feel his hot breath as he hovers, not quite touching me. Suddenly, he is everywhere at once, his nails scraping firmly down my body, his mouth, kissing, licking and biting. My thighs, my legs, my belly, and my arms. I'm so surprised I buck violently. I scream, not in pain, though I feel a bit of that, but more from the shock of it. And just as sudden as this assault to my senses has started, it has stopped. He moves away quickly and without my sight, it feels like I am alone. My breathing is heavy and labored. I need to calm myself. Just as I am beginning to breathe easily again, I feel his mouth on that oh so sweet spot in the center of me. He latches on with tremendous strength as if he is trying to devour me. My clit pulses and pounds. All the while his hands move slowly, so very slowly up and down my legs and belly. The alternate sensations are spiking my pleasure to the point of ecstasy. The pressure is too much, yet not quite enough. I hover on the brink of intense orgasm. I don't tip over. I need... Something more. I feel his laughter against my mound. He knows what he's doing to me. He is holding me at the brink but not letting me fall. He moves away again. This goes on for what seems like forever. Greg, building my pleasure to the point of excruciating pain and then, stopping. When he stops, he moves away from me completely, and I am deprived of any sensation but the breeze in the room touching my body all over, reminding me of how I am not being touched at all. Tears stream down my cheeks.

"Please!?" I beg. The music still swells so loud that I cannot hear a reply to my pleading.

Greg returns to me again heading right for my very core licking gently and lazily. Has no intention of letting me come. I don't think I can take much more of it. I don't know what he's trying to prove. My face is soaking wet with tears of frustration now. "Greg, please! Please! Please!" My pleading becomes a mantra. All the while he laps playfully at my folds, nips at my inner thighs, and his hands gently create patterns, softly stroking the flesh of my arms and belly. I understand now. At least I think I do.

"Greg?" He pauses and I can feel him looking up at me, though I cannot see him.

"Lollipop."

Using his hands to spread me, two fingers spear my now swollen folds, and he begins to pump me forcefully, repeatedly jabbing that oh so wonderful spot inside me while his lips latch onto my clit, giving me just what I need, the perfect speed and pressure to tip... over the edge. My orgasm is long and loud and glorious. His movements slow as I float back from heaven on a cloud of joy. His stroking slows, yet his kisses continue at the apex of my thighs and up and down my legs. I am complete jelly now. Now that I'm returning to my body I feel his arms massaging my legs, and I notice the stiffness, having been clenching my thighs and legs for so long. He kisses and rubs my legs and brings the blood flow back to my limbs. The music slowly ebbs to nothingness, and I hear his murmur of appreciation.
"That's it Katy baby, let it all out." Have I been crying this entire time? I know I screamed when my climax finally took me. What this is now is simply a series of sobs. I am sobbing now. And I feel... so, so good… Free.

I wake with a start. I am boiling. And I can see the reason why now. Greg is wrapped around me like a monkey on a tree, hanging on for dear life. His head rests in the crook of my armpit, his hand rest on my belly and his large, heavy thigh lay across my legs pinning me down. I fidget trying to readjust myself and get comfortable.

"I love you, Kaitlin." What? I look down at him, touching his face. Greg flinches as if something is irritating him. He's asleep. Thank God. I know I feel something for him, a lot more than I was hoping to, really... But love? He's way too fast. Thank God, thank God, thank God he's asleep. Oh well, I'll enjoy knowing his little secret. I snuggle in, my sated body searching for the other half of it's spoon.

"Wake up sleepy head. Pizza!"

Continued in Billionaire Boyfriend...

Thank you for reading!

If You like my work, please take a minute to write a review.

Visit my website and sign up for exclusive content, updates and FREEBIES!

ELYSEYOUNG.COM

Manufactured by Amazon.ca
Acheson, AB